D1420884

BAXTER

Vs.

THE BOOKIES

RACING STORIES

by

ROY GRANVILLE

Roy Granville

Illustrations by LEZZ

Published by
Hayes Press
PO Box 489
Hayes
UB3 2WZ

First published in Great Britain in 2004 by
Hayes Press
PO Box 489
Hayes
UB3 2WZ

A CIP catalogue number is available from the British Library.

ISBN 0-9548604-0-3

Typeset by Simpson Drewett, Richmond, Surrey.
Printed and bound in Great Britain by CPD, Wales.

Horses are rather nice, silly, harmless creatures if they were only left to mind their own business.

Basil Boothroyd

"It's out again on Tuesday, shall I book you for the ride?"

CONTENTS

A PLACE TO BE FILLED

Baxter had a toothache. He put it down to an inadequate brush whose bristles resembled a Grand National hedge after the second circuit and too many rich tea fingers. However, when he rang Parnell's surgery he was told his dentist of 30 years had retired.

"He never mentioned that last time I came" said Baxter slightly miffed but at the same time puzzled that a man who had listened so attentively to his tips could afford to retire. "Probably never backed 'em" mumbled Baxter in an effort to explain the anomaly.

"Would you like an appointment with Mr Quinn who's taken over?"

The receptionist's question reminded him that he was still on the phone.

"Any good is he?" asked Baxter.

"Oh yes, he's Australian" said the girl, seeming to Baxter to contradict herself.

"Book me in tomorrow" he said. "Must be the morning though."

"I'm afraid the earliest he can see you is in three weeks - he's fully-booked until then."

"Look, I don't want a transplant" pointed out Baxter "a filling would probably do it."

Having declined to wait the three weeks, Baxter hoped the toothache would pass and decided to rely on the codeine tablets supplied to him by Mrs Wilbow, his office landlady. "She's not a bad old stick" he conceded, popping a tablet into his mouth. "Ought to try and bring her rent up to date one day." This, however, was only a fleeting thought before sanity returned.

Besides, he was going to need all his funds because an unusual situation had arisen with regard to one of his Newmarket contacts who had invited him to take part in a coup. Normally, Baxter would have accepted the offer with the alacrity of a desert nomad being offered a pint of beer but the coup was basically to get the horse placed and back it each-way.

Like most professionals, Baxter only backed to win. Each-way betting occasionally had its merits but in Baxter's opinion it generally enabled you to do twice your money in half the time. However, this particular contact was highly regarded by Baxter and the stable knew the time of day. The circumstances of the race also meant it would be difficult to get the money down but the unrivalled pleasure of slapping the bookies was irresistible and he was in.

The race selected for the coup was a novice handicap chase at Kempton Park on the Saturday. As a rule, such a race would receive a swerve as wide as the Queen Mary from Baxter but, on analysis, it was not a competitive race at all. The favourite looked good, had won its last two chases impressively and would start about 3's on. The other entries were a mixture of bad horses, chancy jumpers and horses making their debut over fences.

The subject of the gamble was a horse named

Long Shorts who was a reasonable jumper but hadn't raced for nearly a year. The plan was that the horse would definitely get in the first three and, if the favourite failed, might even win. With an anticipated S.P. of 10-1, it was a knocking bet to delight any reputable thief.

On the Thursday there was the dead eight entered and the problem was that any non-runner would confine the places to two. A phone call to the plotters was re-assuring.

"Don't worry, we'll take care of that - eight runners is what there'll be."

Baxter's study of the form was also encouraging. Although the favourite looked nailed on, the second favourite was a decent hurdler who may or may not jump the bigger obstacles. Two of them should have been registered at Cruft's rather than Weatherby's, and another two could probably have fallen over hopscotch lines. That left a soured 8-year-old who was as genuine as a digital watch by Tompion and, of course, Long Shorts.

On Friday afternoon, Baxter had availed himself of his overdraft facility and had £1000 in twenty-pound notes on his desk. However, even the pleasure of this rare sight could not overcome the nagging pain inside his mouth.

There was a knock at the door and, seeing the unmistakable outline of Mrs Wilbow through the frosted glass, he opened a drawer and swept the money into it.

Baxter coughed.

"Hello, Mrs Wilbow, I'll be settling up with you soon."

"It's giving me hell, Mrs Wilbow"

"I've not come about that although it would be nice to get paid" she said. "No, I've come to see how your toothache was."

"It's giving me hell, Mrs Wilbow."

"Yes, well I thought as much. You should see a doctor instead of going off racing - you can't keep taking those codeine, you know."

"You're quite right, Mrs Wilbow. I'll sort that out, just as I will the rent." He noticed a couple of the notes had got jammed in the drawer and were flagging their presence so he got up to shepherd her out. "Just how many weeks is it?"

"It's exactly eight this Friday" said the landlady.

"No problem" said Baxter "leave it to me."

He closed the door but not quickly enough to avoid hearing her mumble "I've heard that before."

Mrs Wilbow was right. He needed to see a dentist quickly. Today was already too late but perhaps he could arrange an appointment after racing at Kempton Park the next day. Baxter got hold of the Yellow Pages for the area and telephoned a Dr.Molins in the town.

"Sorry but Dr Molins doesn't work on Saturdays" said the receptionist.

"But this is an emergency" urged Baxter. "I'm coming to the races at Kempton tomorrow, could I see him late afternoon?"

"I'll have a word with him" she said.

She was gone so long, Baxter was questioning whether he'd been cut off or not when her voice came back.

"He said he can see you tomorrow at 5.30 but only as a private patient."

Baxter realised this meant more money but the pain was compelling.

"Great!" he said. "Thank you very much."

It was Saturday and the betting shops opened early which was good because he needed to get the £1000 on in smallish amounts. Long Shorts was to be an S.P. job with no money for it on the course. The Asian mini-cab driver arrived in his Datsun and honked. Baxter went downstairs and was about to get in the back when he found it occupied by children's toys, old newspapers, some tools and a spare tyre.

"Sit here" said a smiling face, indicating the front.

It took Baxter two hours to get the money on, notwithstanding having to take flowery abuse in several shops which included the remarks "At least Dick Turpin wore a mask?", "I thought burglars worked at night" and several requests to perform a task beyond the capabilities of any contortionist.

He paid off the mini-cab at Paddington and hotfooted it to the platform.

The moment he arrived at the course, it started to rain with an intensity that overwhelmed the scant protection his trilby provided. The combination of the pain from his tooth and feeling uncomfortably wet had put him in no mood for punting. He sat in the bar, only wandering out at race time to watch through his binoculars. As the afternoon progressed, he began to notice that the ground was cutting up badly and horses were coming home extremely tired.

A 3-mile novice handicap chase in these conditions was not a race to be involved in but he was - as the bulge of betting slips in his breast pocket confirmed.

The rain was still cascading down but thankfully all eight runners lined up for the final race. Long Shorts price varied between 10's and 12's on the boards as they went off. Baxter's eyes were clamped on Long Shorts and the horse seemed to be jumping well enough in fifth place as they completed the first circuit. The two debutantes had both gone earlier at the same fence but it was on the second circuit that things really started to happen. One of the 'dogs' fell at the open ditch and the other, who had led first time round despite some appalling blunders, unseated his jockey at the water jump. Baxter's impression was that the jockey himself was not averse to the idea.

There were four left with the favourite going easily followed by the ex-hurdler who was safe but deliberate with his jumping. Racing together, a long way behind, came Long Shorts and the antique digital. At the next fence, Long Shorts made a horrible mistake, pitched on landing and stumbled across the path of the other horse that couldn't get out of the way and fell. Had it been a football match, Long Shorts would have been red-carded but it was still there and all it had to do to land the booty was to finish. This wasn't as straightforward as it appeared because Long Shorts had lost its confidence and didn't fancy it much anymore. It was also in need of the race and had become very tired. There were only three to jump and the other two horses were a distance clear. Long Shorts ran down the next fence and just managed to scramble over but was now down to little more than a trot. As it approached the second last it had little momentum to carry it over despite the urgent stoking of the jockey, whose effectiveness compared to a woodpecker with a rubber beak. Baxter felt himself going through a pushing motion in his anxiety to get the horse over. Somehow it scrambled through the brush and just stood there flat out on his feet and snorting frosted puffs of air.

The other two were being led into the unsaddling enclosure as the jockey coaxed Long Shorts into a walk towards the last fence. The importance of finishing in the first three had clearly been impressed on his rider who tried to kick Long Shorts into the fence. Unfortunately, the wretched animal had no more to give and just stopped in front of it. His determined partner turned it round, sat quietly on it for a minute and once more set him towards the obstacle. The crowd had lost interest in what was an excruciating drama to Baxter. People were jostling past him to get home and bookmakers were dismantling their pitches. Baxter had dropped his binoculars and was just staring as Long Shorts approached the fence and again stopped.

Long Shorts, though, was quickly realising that however obvious was its exhaustion and the impossibility of it jumping this fence, his rider was resolutely determined that it should. So it was on the third approach and almost from a standing start that Long Shorts made a final effort and landed on the other side to some derisory applause from the few remaining onlookers.

Baxter had forgotten about his toothache and his dental appointment but with the relief of Long Shorts finishing, he was suddenly reminded of both and hurriedly left the course.

The first thing Baxter noticed about the dentist was that he had protruding ears like little pink loudspeakers on the side of his head. Baxter apologised for being late but said he had been delayed.

The dentist said "No problem, you're my only patient today" and after a brief examination declared a large filling was required.

Not a bad day's work despite everything, thought Baxter as he entered his office. It was dark now and despite still feeling damp he was hungry. However, eating was to be avoided so soon after his extensive re-surfacing so he opted for a glass of Macallan from the bottle in his drawer. After switching on the electric fire, he sat down, removed the bundle of betting slips from his pocket and set them on the table.

He was in much the same situation the next morning because, not for the first time, he had fallen asleep in the office. Mrs Wilbow did not approve of overnight stays so he went noiselessly down the stairs and picked up his 'Racing Post' from the hallway. He had barely returned to his desk when the phone rang.

He picked it up to hear what appeared to be the winning performance in a swearing contest. However, he recognised the voice of his informant from Long Shorts' stable and in between the untranslatable and embittered invective, a shocking truth was emerging.

"But how could only two have finished, I saw Long Shorts cross the line with my own eyes?" asked a disbelieving Baxter. The explanation was followed by another question from Baxter. "You mean, the judge had left his box when it crossed the line and so it couldn't be placed third?"

He started to fidget with the paper which was headlined 'FURORE AT KEMPTON JUDGE'S ABSENCE' and tried to interrupt the continuing tirade booming from his phone.

"But that's disgraceful! Why didn't he stay in his box for heaven's sake? I mean..........."

His voice trailed off as his eyes fell on a small photo below the headline. The face seemed slightly familiar - at least, the protruding ears did.

"Left early to see one of his dental patients, you say?" Baxter felt horribly sick and allowed the phone to slip weakly from his hand. He silently swept the pile of betting slips from his desk to the floor and slumped back in his chair without any appreciation that his toothache had gone.

PERFECT VISION

The proprietor of the SureFire Tipping Service had a new postman. Baxter knew this because his mail was now being delivered at least an hour earlier and, whereas the previous postman had dumped the letters in the downstairs hall, they were now being pushed under his office door. Baxter approved and came face to face with the architect of the improvements when he left his office door ajar. A little man with a tired, sombre face stood there with a huge mail-bag hanging from his neck to his ankles beneath which protruded a pair of small feet.

"Any good at this tipping lark?" he asked Baxter who turned around and smiled at him.

"No, absolute rubbish" said Baxter light-heartedly.

"Yes, I've heard most of them are" said the postman.

"In fact" went on Baxter "this is just a front. I really import rhinoceros, train them up and then hire them out to guard residential premises."

"Oh well, I'll put the word about for you - see if anyone's interested" said the man whose name was Wilfred. He put a small bundle of letters down on the desk.

Baxter was momentarily stunned and realised his attempt at irony had failed as miserably as his recent betting selections.

"No, no, I was joking. Of course, I'm a good tipster - how else could I run a successful business?"

"Don't look all that successful." The postman cast his eyes around the room which was in its usual dilapidated state.

"Well, there are degrees of success" explained Baxter. "I make a living."

"Me, too, but I wouldn't call myself a success" and with that, the animated mailbag shuffled out.

This was Baxter's first encounter with Wilfred but there was something about his downtrodden lugubrious nature that appealed and he deliberately left his door ajar so as to have a chat when the little man came.

It was in October, a couple of days after the accident. Wilfred's feet had become entangled with the mailbag on some stairs and after some wild gyrations with his arms and some loud shrieking, he'd finally landed but not without some damage to his back. When Wilfred next arrived, the strap on the mailbag had been considerably shortened.

"How's the back?" asked Baxter.

"Bloomin' painful" said Wilfred.

"No line-dancing for you then" teased Baxter.

"No, never been interested in that" said Wilfred seriously. "Probably be no good at it, anyway."

Baxter's mail was becoming very meagre of late. There were two letters recognisable as bills and one other.

"This one's addressed to 'THE IDIOT' but I reckon it's for you" said Wilfred helpfully.

"This one's addressed to 'The Idiot'"

"Yes, thanks" acknowledged Baxter. "Some people can be very abusive where money is involved and, to tell the truth, I'm badly out of form. What I wouldn't give for a winner."

"Well, I reckon Toasted Spider will win today. Now where was I?" Wilfred paused and scratched the side of his head. "Pontefract I think it was - is there a meeting there today?"

"There is but that rag, Toasted Spider, can't win. If you got Mike Tyson to chase me, I could beat that!"

"Only trying to help" said Wilfred leaving. "That's what was in the dream."

"A dream!" derided Baxter. "When I start believing in them, I'll shoot myself!" The door closed and Baxter applied himself to the study of the form-book. An hour passed but he had no confidence in himself or his contacts. The message to his clients would have to be 'no selection today'.

It was fortunate for Baxter that he didn't possess a gun for Toasted Spider had won. Even if he had, he would have excused himself on the grounds that Mrs Wilbow already complained about the room being a mess. Finding his dead body, would have been the last straw. Besides, Toasted Spider had only won because the other five runners had taken the wrong course and it had been too far behind to follow them. On the other hand, a winner was a winner and the new racing sage was warmly welcomed the following morning.

"That was some winner you dreamt up yesterday, Wilfred. I didn't know you were interested in racing."

"I'm not really but I did think of being a jockey as a kid - being small like - but here I am, a postman."

"And a very good one" offered Baxter. "So how long have you been dreaming these winners?"

"That was the first" said Wilfred whose drawn face looked as if it were suspending weights. "See, my back's so bad I can't sleep so I study a race-card and that gives me something to think about. Then when I do go off, I imagine I'm at the races. Sort of hallu.....helloose..."

"Hallucinating?" prompted Baxter.

"That's it" nodded Wilfred. "It's the drugs that do it."

"You're into drugs?" Baxter was shocked.

"Yes, well when I went to the hospital about my back, they asked me if I would take part in a clinical trial for a new drug. They can't do much for back pain, you know, but these tablets are supposed to work. You take them at night because they make you drowsy but I reckon they also give you these hallu.... hallucinations."

"Could be" said Baxter. "Did you dream anything last night?"

"I did but I forget where I was. All I know is that I was riding this horse and this other jockey came by me in the last 50 yards and beat me half a length."

"You were unlucky" offered Baxter, entering into the spirit of things. "Maybe the horse had made a bad jump earlier."

"No" said slumberland's jockey "he jumped

well - I just wasn't strong enough at the finish."

"Well, you've got a bad back" sympathised Baxter. "The problem is identifying the swine who beat you?"

"He was short" said Wilfred, not meaning to be unhelpful "and he had a face like a weasel."

This was also unhelpful because all jockeys were shifty-looking to Baxter. He just wished he had a rogue's gallery for Wilfred to study. However, they were in luck because lying on the desk was the 'Racing Post' and suddenly Wilfred was pointing at a photo of a jockey.

"That's him! That's the one."

Baxter recognised the ugly dial and fortunately he was down for just one ride at Bangor.

"Great!" he exclaimed and immediately set up his tipping line with the words "After painstaking research....." which was at least true on Wilfred's part.

As the little fellow turned to go, Baxter said "I hope you backed Toasted Spider yesterday."

"Oh, no" said Wilfred " I wouldn't back any of them."

Baxter admonished him. "It's a waste of talent."

"I just want to get better" said Wilfred which was curious to Baxter because the mailbag was now pulled so tight that he seemed in the process of hanging himself.

The next month was the most glorious run in Baxter's career. Winner after winner flowed unerringly from the SureFire Tipping Service and all revealed by the hallucinatory effects of the tablets. Wilfred studied a particular card, and was there either as a jockey, spectator and, even once, as a steward which Baxter thought extremely useful in the case of objections.

It was a golden period of winners from even money to 33 to 1 and Baxter's advertising was now up to full-page displays of strident copy which could have taught Mr Barnum a thing or two. New subscribers were pouring in and extra phone lines installed to cope with demand.

The only hiccup was on a particular cold morning when Wilfred met Baxter's overjoyous greeting with "Haven't got one today."

Baxter was mortified.

"Racing's off at Ayr" explained the visionary.

"Off? But the inspection's not for another hour.......oh-h-h." Baxter's voice trailed off before picking up again. "So why didn't you study the all-weather card at Lingfield instead? What a let-down!"

"What about me! I went all the way up to Ayr for nothing." responded Wilfred.

Baxter gave him a funny look but insisted that if a meeting was ever in doubt, the all-weather card was to be the choice for bedtime study.

Apart from this, it was all honey. Baxter was backing the selections with absolute confidence, his betting bank was showing explosive growth and his dream of retirement to the country, with a small-holding and a couple of ex-racehorses for company was looking to come true. Wilfred, on the other hand, was untouched by the success. While he never backed the horses, neither did he resent the exploitation of the phenomenon. Money seemed of little interest to Wilfred and the situation troubled Baxter's generous nature. However, he did pay for Wilfred and his wife to spend two weeks in Scarborough and regularly sent her flowers and chocolates. It never seemed quite enough to Baxter but his dilemma was suddenly resolved when the little man gave a rare smile and announced to Baxter.

"My back problem's been cured. It's taken a long time but the tablets have finally worked. Yesterday evening all the pain disappeared - just like that! Bloomin' amazing."

"That's great" said Baxter warmly but unaware what the news implied.

"What a sleep I had!" Wilfred smiled again, this time revealing teeth - the novelty of which disconcerted Baxter.

"And so what bookie-busting beauty have we come up with? I think we agreed to go to Wolverhampton" he said in an effort to get on with the day's business.

Wilfred shook his head. "All that stuff is finished now. I threw the rest of the tablets away. I don't need them anymore."

"What! You can't stop now!" protested Baxter. "You're a walking gold mine! Couldn't you get some more from the doctor and take them anyway?"

"But that would be silly."

Baxter robust frame felt suddenly hollow.

"Silly?" he said weakly. "There'll never be an

opportunity like this again. Don't you want to be rich?"

"No" said Wilfred "too much worry, I reckon."

Baxter was in despair and he wasn't sure what to do. His reliance on the postman meant that he'd neglected his contacts and didn't even study form any-more. There seemed little point when the little man could hand him winners on a plate.

A period of famine descended. Winners became elusive and the clients deserted in droves. He did try to get Wilfred to change his mind but it was difficult to argue with innocence and Baxter eventual-ly regained his equanimity. He'd had a good run and now it was back to normal. The uncharitable thought that Wilfred's back problems might return did occasionally enter his head but he stood back from schemes to get Wilfred to help move his desk or of placing dangerous obstacles on the stairs.

And then it happened. It was March when Wilfred's back went again. He was in the habit of using the banister rail to haul himself up the stairs and Mrs Wilbow must have overdone the polishing. He'd lost his grip and gone crashing down.

"Of course, I'll go back to the old treatment" said Wilfred to Baxter's urgent questioning. "Did me the world of good before."

Baxter was so grateful to Mrs Wilbow that he paid up his rent arrears and complimented her on her polishing. The timing was also quite perfect for Cheltenham was just around the corner and Baxter wondered what he'd done to deserve such good fortune. He reckoned it might have been the copy of 'War Cry' he'd bought or the donation of some old racing books to the church bazaar.

The next morning Baxter was tingling with excitement. The SureFire Tipping Service had been primed ready for action and he was just waiting for the ammunition to arrive.

Wilfred appeared looking more doleful than usual - a countenance only comparable with that of course students in grief and miserabilism.

"Doctor can't give me any more of them tablets" he said.

"Why not?" asked Baxter trying to combine concern with horror.

"They failed the clinical tests - they've been withdrawn."

"Failed? Withdrawn?" echoed Baxter. "How could they have failed - they worked wonders for both of us."

"Oh, they cleared up the back pain alright but people complained about the hallucinations. That's what got them banned, the doctor called it 'damaging side effects'."

Baxter was on that hysterical edge between comedy and tragedy.

"Damaging!" he howled. "Damaging! The only damage they did was to bookmakers and who cares about them!"

THE ARTFUL DODGER

Striving horses with necks outstretched, thrusting jockeys, flailing whips and the sound of thudding hooves on turf – all part of a stirring drama as six of the runners in the 4.30 at Newmarket passed the post in a bunch finish.

This splendid piece of handicapping held no excitement for Baxter, however, because he had backed the only other runner that was now trailing in some ten lengths behind the others.

Baxter muttered a variety of oaths as he tore up and discarded his betting ticket. It was surprising to some racegoers the amount of violence and energy Baxter could employ in the performance of disposing of a piece of paper. It was quite unrivalled and almost artistic in its execution but Baxter took no credit for this except that he'd had an unwelcome amount of practice at it.

As the horses came off the course towards the unsaddling enclosure, he spotted Percy de Montfort looking very belligerent and leaning forward to shout at the rider of Baxter's unfortunate choice.

"Call yourself a jockey?" shouted Percy. "You couldn't sit on a bus!"

Baxter was acquainted with Percy de Montfort as were most racecourse regulars. A confirmed gambler, Percy, at twenty one, had inherited a small fortune plus a stately home from an uncle and seemed intent on using such to provide a transfusion of funds to the already robust satchels of bookmakers.

"Back it did you, Percy?" asked Baxter sympathetically.

"A monkey I had on it, that's how much" snapped Percy as the horse and rider passed in front of him.

"A monkey!" echoed Baxter.

Percy nodded towards the jockey.

"Yes, two counting him!"

The jockey looked back indignantly at his critic.

"It's alright, there's nothing else behind you!" called Percy, continuing the attack. He gazed hostility at the retreating duo before turning glumly to Baxter. "My banker for the day that was."

"Mine too" replied Baxter, reflecting that his SureFire Tipping Service was sounding off an unbelievable number of blanks lately.

"You here for the Cambridgeshire tomorrow?" asked Percy.

"Yes, I'll stay on" said Baxter "might hear something."

"Listen, if you can meet me in the Horse and Groom tomorrow at twelve, I could have some information for you" said Percy, throwing his nose into a large white handkerchief.

"You've caught a cold" observed Baxter.

"You can say that alright" said Percy unhappily.

He watched the plump figure swagger off in its camel coat and brown trilby.

"The odd silver candlestick in a bookmaker's satchel"

"The Horse and Groom at twelve then" he called after it.

Just then, the result of the photo was announced and greeted with whoops of delight from the bookies because the outsider of the field had got it. Smiling faces with busy hands were already dismantling the bookies' joints. Wispy blue smoke from fat Havana cigars drifted towards the darkening sky. Soon the old enemy would be on their way to the bar to congratulate themselves or off home in Rollers like Vikings returning from a pillage. It was a hopeless battle and yet Baxter dreamed ….one day ….. one day.

Even now there was promise for Percy de Montfort was not an entire fool. Reckless in his gambling perhaps but he did have the acquaintance of jockeys and trainers and did get genuine information. Percy's trouble was that he was impulsive and bet far too often which made him fodder for the bookies and put him under considerable financial pressure. He'd already had the grounds of his stately home cemented to cut gardening costs and it wasn't unknown for the odd tiara or silver candlestick to find its way into a bookie's satchel.

Baxter's only misgiving was why Percy should want to share his information with him but put it down to racing camaraderie and a mutual desire to slaughter a bookmaker.

The wind coursed down Newmarket High Street stinging Baxter's face, swirled around the flapping bottom of his raincoat and buffeted his progress to the Horse and Groom. He had just saved his hat from being blown off yet again when he heard his name called. Percy de Montfort was standing in a doorway on the other side of the road.

"I thought you said the Horse and Groom" said Baxter when he'd crossed over.

"I did" said Percy "but I've got some business to attend to and I'm a bit pushed for time. You'd better come in with me."

Baxter entered a low-beamed corridor just wide enough to afford passage to Percy's great bulk. At the end was a large hall in which a sale of antiques appeared to be taking place. Percy grabbed two chairs at the end of a row and motioned to Baxter.

"We'll have to be quiet" he warned "but there's a nice item here and I don't want to miss it."

Baxter sat down, not at all interested in the sale but waiting patiently for Percy's precious words of information. At last Percy coughed to attract his attention.

"You know 'Wing Nuts' Wilson in Nathan's yard?"

Baxter nodded. There was a pause before Percy continued quietly.

"A good judge wouldn't you say, knows what he's talking about?"

Again Baxter nodded, at the same time noticing that Percy would occasionally raise a pen to his nose.

"Well, he told me in confidence this morning but I know I can trust you to keep it quiet."

Baxter nodded keenly to confirm this erroneous judgement.

"Gay Lady has been well tried and the stable won't hear of defeat – help yourself to it."

Baxter's feeling on receipt of the news was distinctly lukewarm. It was rather like expecting the magician to produce a rabbit from the hat when all he produces is a label bearing the hat size. Gay Lady had not needed any tipping, was already 4 to 1 clear favourite and, in Baxter's opinion, terrible value for a race such as the Cambridgeshire.

However, his disappointment was interrupted by a truck-size man with the nose of a truffle hog and the eyes of a scrutineer, who leaned down towards him.

"Could I have your name and address, sir?"

"What for?" said Baxter puzzled.

"I think you just bought that oil painting he's holding" said Percy helpfully. "It must have been those nods you kept giving."

"Cheque or cash, sir?" asked the man. "We also need your address to arrange dispatch."

"But I don't want an oil painting, you know that" argued Baxter.

"Yes" said Percy getting up "but he looks a bad-tempered type, it might be wiser to pay up. Anyway, I've got to go. See you at the course."

Baxter turned to the man still hovering above him.

"Look, there's been a mistake."

The narrow eyes almost came together.

"Mistake, sir? Would you come to the office then?" he added gruffly.

The distance to the office was very short

indeed but on reaching it, Baxter decided that a change of attitude was in his interest.

"How much am I supposed to have bid for the painting?" he asked.

The man propped it up against the desk.

"Two hundred guineas, sir. Look very nice over the fireplace."

"Look better in it" retorted Baxter. "Two hundred guineas for that!"

The picture scowling back at Baxter was of an old buffer in uniform decorated with scrambled egg and ribboned gongs and with the look of a favourite punter who had just seen it pipped on the line by a 20 to 1 shot.

Outside the auctioneers, Baxter gave a deep sigh and a shrug of his shoulders. He was more than £200 down before racing had started and all he had to show for it was a piece of uninspiring information. He decided to ring his office and have Gay Lady sent out to subscribers but only because he could think of no better alternative.

It was finding the big price winners that pulled the punters in, as Baxter well knew, whereas short-priced winners were easy to find – at least, that's what the uneducated believed. If only they were right, reflected Baxter, he would be a millionaire.

There was a springer in the market for the Cambridgeshire that afternoon. The horse called Watering Weeds was a sustained gamble from 20's down to 5's and although Baxter didn't fancy it, the trainer was a man who, when it came to conspiracies, would have run rings around Machiavelli. Gay Lady had now drifted to 8's and Baxter had a pony on it but without much confidence.

From the stands, Baxter watched the huge field set off and it was only from about two furlongs out that the grip on his bins grew significantly tighter as he saw how well Gay Lady was travelling. Taking it up from the distance, the ante-post favourite went a couple of lengths clear before Watering Weeds came through with a late challenge. Although it was a photo, Baxter never had any doubts that Gay Lady had held on.

He went down to the unsaddling enclosure. Percy was there, red-faced, plenty of blood pressure.

"Don't worry, Percy, we've got it!"

"Oh" said Percy nervously "which one's got it, d'you think?"

"Our one of course – Gay Lady. Only a head in it maybe but the springer never quite got up." Just then the announcement of the photo confirmed that Baxter was right. "There you are, Percy. Good price in the end as well!"

"Oh, go jump in the river" said Percy angrily and pushed himself through the crowd.

It was pretty strange behaviour, thought Baxter, but was only slightly distracted from his immediate objective. He strode off towards the line of bookmakers holding his betting ticket. He was off to collect some blood.

Baxter spent a pleasant weekend knowing that not only had he covered expenses but that Gay Lady's win would encourage more hopeful but deluded supporters for his tipping service. It was only Percy de

Montfort's behaviour that bothered him for it appeared that he had backed the beaten horse, in which case, why had he bothered to arrange to tell Baxter about Gay Lady?

The explanation arrived on Monday morning with the delivery of the unwanted picture. As Baxter was deciding which part of the office to discard it to, he became aware that certain lines of the puffy pace were familiar. When he turned the frame over there was a small inscription - 'To my dear nephew, Percy, from Brigadier Samuel de Montfort'.

THE DIFFERENCE A DAY MAKES

Like a sea captain about to study his charts, Baxter prepared for his morning perusal of the racing press. He cleared a large central area on his battered desk which meant that various bills, letters, pencils, old race cards and other impedimenta were swept overboard to join other flotsam on the floor of his office.

He laid the paper out before him and then brought over his cup of coffee and two rich tea fingers and placed them along its right hand edge. He sat down, gave a resigned grunt and absently dunked a biscuit into the brown liquid.

Reading reviews of the previous day's racing was becoming akin to studying autopsy reports as far as Baxter's recent selections were concerned. His mood was less than benevolent.

He mashed at the biscuit, ruminating with cynicism as he read the report on two of the beaten favourites. The writer was either extremely naive or a practising Christian felt Baxter, for he could find nothing to confirm his own suspicion that, in at least one case, the jockey had been 'at it'.

His eyes roved across to another column where a picture of a trainer with a big hat, prying nose and shifty eyes, reminded him of that other group of bandits roaming racetracks. Mentally he drew several vertical steel bars over the unprepossessing face and decided the defacement suited George 'Washington' Croker admirably.

George Croker had been dubbed 'Washington' with some irony because whereas the old statesman had been reckoned never to tell a lie, Croker was universally felt never to have told a truth - at least, not as far as his horses were concerned. Croker, for his part, seemed unperturbed by the insinuation and claimed to have a great admiration for the original 'G.W.' even to the extent of having a portrait of the old boy above his fireplace.

However, the fact was that George 'Washington' Croker was the arch exponent of stroke-pulling and if Baxter had been pressed to construct an all-aged handicap of villains of the turf, 'G.W' Croker would have had top weight of 12 stone. In the race proper, he would have had the worst of the draw, been ridden by an amateur putting up overweight, would have started at fours on, would have never been off the bit and won in a common canter by ten lengths.

Such a high rating was well-earned for the racing intelligentsia had long since given up trying to fathom the devious workings of his mind. The in and out form shown by his runners was borne out by the fact that in accounting for such to the stewards, 'G.W' Croker had told more stories than the 'Arabian Nights'.

His favourite ploy was to run two or three horses in the same race and invariably put his best jockey on the one with the least form. Form students had been known to seek asylum from races in which Croker had runners and they were generally entertained only by masochists. Racing scribes fared no better. When asked which of his runners was the more fancied, he either gave an inscrutable look, answered ambiguously or simply lied.

Bookies, too, were wary of Croker's horses for when he did back one on the course which got beat by one of his other runners, their satisfaction was often short-lived when they learned that he'd landed a nice touch in their betting shops with some late money for the winner. In essence, 'G.W' Croker was a slippery customer and not one to meddle with.

If, on the other hand, Baxter reasoned, one could solve the devious workings of such a mind, an avenue of rich opportunity peopled by weeping bookies stretched before you.

He turned to the probables for Saturday and noted that 'G.W' Croker had three runners in a tricky handicap at Sedgefield. As 'G.W' trained at Elmslea, which was an hour from London and a long way from Sedgefield, it was a tip in itself.

Baxter could be oddly impulsive at times. It was this and the additional stupefying effects of a couple of malt whiskies that found him on the milk train to Elmslea. What he quite hoped to gain from his visit, he wasn't quite sure. Perhaps he hoped to ingratiate himself with 'G.W' or perhaps he wanted to get away from the pageantry of racing for a moment and see it in its crudity and preparation.

Whatever it was, there was no taxi waiting when he arrived. The sky was grey and brooding and a glistening coat of frost covered the grass by the side of the road.

It was brass-monkey weather all right, complained Baxter as he set off towards the gallops - although somewhat unreasonably, as it was the first week in February.

He reached a line of well-used ground by the side of which sat Croker on his hack, watching his string work by in pairs.

Baxter turned his cold face upwards.

"Morning G.W" he said cheekily.

"Morning" said the trainer with a mere glimpse and much reserve.

"I'm Binns, the new chap on 'Horses and Form' explained Baxter. "Wonder if you can tell us anything about your chances for the handicap at Sedgefield on Saturday."

"Did you?" he said emptily. There was a silence apart from the rise and fall of drumming hooves across the turf. "You must be keen" he said at last "you're the first I've seen on the gallops. Most of you fellows ask such questions on the phone." He still wasn't looking at Baxter. "I expect you'll soon be like the rest of 'em."

The short figure of a work rider approached them. He was leading a plain-looking horse that was obviously feeling himself. He led the horse in front of Croker and pointed to a front leg.

"Must 'ave rapped himself, guvnor."

The trainer dismounted and bent down to look at the bloodied cut.

"Say, isn't that Village Emperor?" said Baxter of the horse he had the misfortune to back several times.

"It might be, might not."

"Not likely to be going to Sedgefield then?"

"We don't know yet, we could still have him ready" offered Croker. Yes, about as much chance as seeing the Queen in a tattooist's, thought Baxter.

"Might see you at Sedgefield then." The tone was dismissive. "Sorry I can't be more helpful" Croker smiled thinly.

Baxter returned to his office feeling the trip had been as fruitful as an empty banana. All he'd learned was that Croker would have only two runners at Sedgefield and that his reputation for being evasive was well-deserved. It certainly hadn't made it any easier to arrive at his Saturday nap - the good thing that would placate the unrest amongst his clients, the majority of whom, even he admitted, were showing remarkable fortitude in the current run of absolute stumers.

After many hours of studying, Baxter was almost embarrassed by his final selection. He could imagine the groans and derisory remarks when his clients received it - an obvious favourite at Sandown, selected by all the newspapers, likely to start at odds on and which would probably tip over at the first. But confidence was low - it wasn't a time to take chances.

It was a relief when someone on the train to Sedgefield told him that Sandown had been called off after an inspection. At least the clients couldn't blame him for that and he could now devote himself to deciding which of 'G.W.' Croker's runners was the one to be on.

Of the two, Baxter felt that Hammersmith

had the better form but now saw from the paper that the stable jockey was riding the other one named Shampoo. Baxter felt a headache coming on.

There were 12 runners for the 2 mile handicap hurdle but such esteem was Croker held in that the bookies went 5/4, 7/4 his pair and 10 bar. There was no value in betting the pair so it became imperative that Baxter got a pointer from Croker in one direction. From there he could go fearlessly in the opposite knowing that 'G.W' always lied or misinformed as a matter of course.

He saw the trainer in the middle of the parade ring surrounded by the two jockeys, the owners and their friends. If Baxter could have read the frosted breath from Croker's mouth he would have been home and dried but he could only watch the arch conspirator at work and his only sure knowledge was that 'G.W' had the race well and truly sewn up.

The horses were starting to leave the paddock. Baxter stared at the 7lb claiming jockey on Hammersmith, examining his face for any tell-tale clue but discovered only that the boy had a bad case of acne. Time was short - something had to be done. He pushed his way through the crowd and caught Croker's arm.

"Afternoon G.W" he said breathlessly. "Remember me?"

Croker turned and looked unusually affable. "I do - Binns wasn't it?"

"That's right" said Baxter. "Look, could you put me right on your two runners here? They're a bit close in the market."

"Undoubtedly useless – probably rode like a Cherokee brave"

Croker smiled benignly. "I'll just say that the lad is good value for his claim and that could give Hammersmith the edge."

"Thanks G.W" yelped Baxter and charged off to the ring.

Knowing that Croker was out to mislead him, he could see it all so clearly. The claimer was undoubtedly useless - probably rode like a Cherokee brave attacking a wagon train - and the stable jockey would trot up on Shampoo. Hammersmith was now down to evens on the boards and they'd got 'G.W' all wrong again, mused Baxter as he availed himself of plenty of 2 to 1 about Shampoo.

It certainly looked that way in the race with Shampoo taking it up two hurdles out and going well and Hammersmith in the middle of the chasing pack. It was then that Baxter witnessed an admirable piece of riding which he didn't quite appreciate for Hammersmith was suddenly brought up sweetly to challenge the leader and popped neatly over the last to win by an easy 4 lengths.

Baxter was stunned. He didn't know how it had all gone wrong but it had and any further thought of 'G.W' Croker was nauseating. He was shuffling disconsolately towards the exit when he heard Croker call to him.

"All right, Binns?" he said pleasantly.

"All right, you twister! I would have been if I'd backed Hammersmith" wailed Baxter.

"But I told you. I said to be on Hammersmith" said the trainer incredulously.

"Yes and when did you ever tell the truth?"

countered Baxter.

"Ah, I take your point" 'G.W' nodded "but one must have a little respect for one's hero and today you could trust me completely."

Baxter didn't understand so the trainer went on. "You see, today is the 22nd of February."

"I know that" retorted Baxter.

"But you obviously don't know that it's also George Washington's birthday" smiled Croker.

THE LONELY HEARTS WHEEZE

The atmosphere on the race-train returning from Bath was subdued. The shortest-priced winner on the whole card had been 10-1 and the results may just as well have been composed by The Society of Bookmakers. Baxter immersed himself in a corner and tried to block his mind from the afternoon's events. He fidgeted as though endeavouring to sink himself further into the seat and have the upholstery envelop him completely for he wished to disappear from view.

The reason was that a number of racegoers were well aware that Baxter was the proprietor of the SureFire Tipping Service, a fact that was, at present, causing him acute embarrassment.

One of the truisms in racing was that to back odds-on chances was a sure way to the poorhouse. However, Baxter clients were starting to feel they had discovered a shortcut.

The subject of money raised all sorts of emotions but losing it, predominantly raised one – anger. Baxter hid behind the spread-eagled pages of his 'Racing Post' while bemoaning the demise of 'The Sporting Life' whose broadsheets would have offered far better cover.

If only someone had invented a spray which would render one invisible whenever it was required.

Crikey! They would have made a fortune, reckoned Baxter. He certainly could have used a can at the moment and saved himself a lot of cautious eye-swivelling.

Alternatively, he could have used it to arrive at Martin Pipe's Nicholshayne stable, slipped into the house and then headed for the kitchen where he would have heard all the plotting that went on over the toast and marmalade. In the summer, he'd have sauntered into Henry Cecil's rose garden and fallen in behind as Henry discussed a horse's chance with its owner. The trainer's fondness for a smoke also meant that Baxter could have had one at the same time without raising suspicion. Still, other people would probably have the same idea and you'd end up with dozens of invisible people bumping into each other and giving Henry the right hump. Baxter abandoned the scheme as flawed but the principle of invisibility unquestionably held some appeal.

Thankfully, he arrived at Paddington without abuse or injury and took a taxi home. Of course, it was the failure of his racing contacts that had brought upon this feeling of vulnerability and the depressing fact was that they had all become unreliable at the same time. He had to recruit some new contacts that were both sound and astute – commodities that were as hard to find as a smile on a murder victim.

Baxter's lack of interest in the opposite sex was long established but this did not prevent him from occasionally browsing through the Lonely Hearts columns of his local paper. He found it quite amusing that 'Wealthy Banker, Tall, Elegant with Film-Star looks and charisma' should need to advertise for a woman. It seemed far more logical that he should require a bouncer to repel hordes of women from beating down his door. The same doubt applied to 'Stunningly Beautiful, Charming, 40 year-old widow with perfect figure' and were both clearly overstatements of their qualities. In truth, it was rather like Baxter's promotion of his SureFire Tipping Service, although this he would have denied.

On this occasion however, his eye caught an advert under the 'WOMEN LOOKING FOR MEN' section. It read:

'Divorced Wife of Ex-Racehorse Trainer seeks Vigorous Man between 40-55. I am attractive, vivacious and will share racing information to our mutual benefit. You should be tall, handsome and know how to treat a woman.'

A premium rate telephone number followed for you to leave a message for the advertiser.

Baxter ran a large circle with his pen around the advert and stared at it. His eyes honed in on the words 'racing information' to the exclusion of all else, particularly the qualities required by the advertiser. He rang the number and after a lengthy preamble to bolster the coffers of the service provider, he was able to leave a message for the woman to call him.

A week went by in which Baxter's fortunes spiralled lower than a snake's belly. He even confided his bad luck to the barman in the Drover's Arms who suggested he must have slept with a witch. Baxter knew that this wasn't the case because he hadn't slept with anyone for aeons, although he declined to confide this fact to the barman.

Baxter had not long been in his office that

morning, when the phone rang. He was rather startled when a woman's voice asked. "Is that William?"

"Er, yes" said Baxter nervously. "Who's this?"

"Clarissa" said a rather nice voice.

"Who?" said Baxter, whose own voice seemed to be drying out.

"Clarissa Reed. You answered my advertisement and left your message on my voice-mail."

"Ah, yes, I'd forgotten about that" said Baxter, who was quite impressed by the soothing tones.

"Unfortunately, I was away when the advert came out and all the other messages got erased by the time I came back. Yours was the only one remaining" she explained.

"So how good's your racing information?" asked Baxter eagerly.

"Oh, it's excellent but don't you want to know more about me?"

Baxter didn't but listened quietly because he knew the woman would tell him anyway.

Clarissa Reed had been married to Jack Reed, an Epsom trainer with a small mixed yard. Baxter had seen him at the races but knew little of him. However, he was obviously an original thinker because he had come up with the novel idea of paying alimony by giving his ex-wife horses to back. On a level stake, the information had run up a profit of £25,000 at which point the trainer gave her no more information until the next annual bout of alimony was due. She went on to say that she was a very attractive, petite blonde with a nice figure. Her two grown-up children no longer lived at home, she was an excellent cook and was keen on all sports, particularly golf and badminton.

But all of the latter information went unnoted by Baxter for he was still thinking about the £25,000 betting profit. Wow! If this was true, he had just discovered the key to the Promised Land.

"Now tell me about yourself" he heard her say. "You're obviously tall and handsome otherwise you wouldn't have answered the advert." She paused. "Would you?"

"That's right" said Baxter awkwardly but all she managed to prise out of him was that he was 5'10" and 13 stone with a clear reluctance to go into more detail as to his appearance.

"So when shall we meet up?" asked the woman.

"Meet up?" repeated Baxter.

"Well, yes. Isn't that the point?" she laughed.

"Oh, that's right" he mumbled "but I'm busy with work at the moment."

"Can I ask you what work you do?" she asked.

"Intelligence" he said cryptically.

"Oh, a sort of James Bond figure" she cooed "you sound very interesting. And are you licensed to thrill?"

Baxter was aware of the woman's charm emanating from the phone but she was a bit too up-front for his comfort. He changed the subject.

"Could you let me know a bit more about the racing information?"

"You sound more interested in that than in me" she sighed. "Actually, I do have one today. It's the start of our financial year so I expect there will be quite

"You're obviously tall and handsome!"

a bit in the coming weeks. Jack likes to meet the target figure quickly so he doesn't have to bother with me for a while. Does that make sense?"

"Well, yes" said Baxter, thinking it couldn't be that easy to find winners "but you must have some losers?"

"Not so far" said Clarissa "I'd be very upset if that happened."

Twenty-five grand of profit and no losers, thought Baxter – it sounded impossible! She then gave him the name of Interesting Ant running at Newton Abbot and promised to ring him again when she hoped they could meet up.

When Baxter looked at the Newton Abbot race, he wasn't particularly impressed. It was a selling race over 2 miles with just 5 runners and Interesting Ant was forecast to start at evens.

Baxter's clients didn't like short priced tips, believing they could pick that sort of thing out for themselves. Baxter didn't care much for them either because when they won the re-action he got was 'Big deal! It was entitled to win at that price!' and when they got beat he was castigated for tipping such a short-priced loser.

However, these were desperate times so Interesting Ant went up on his tipping line and as Baxter was going to be at Lingfield at the time of the race, he rang up his credit account and had £250 on the beast.

His visit to Lingfield turned out to be more of a scouting mission. There were a few whispers on the course but not from anyone he gave much credence to and he confined himself to noting a couple of horses unlucky in running and several 157's who were being laid out for better things.

Shortly after 4 o'clock, he walked into the course betting shop to find Interesting Ant had indeed won but with two non-runners in the race the starting price had been 4's on. Already he could hear the mental hoots of derision and the spluttering of drinks his clients might be holding when they heard the price.

Clarissa rang the next day. The purring tones from the phone were such that Baxter felt inclined to stroke it.

"I've got another one for you, William. Aren't you a lucky man!"

"Bit short, aren't they?" said Baxter ungratefully.

"Short?"

"Yes, the price – I'm not going to get fat on them."

"Yes, I do understand but they probably wouldn't win if they weren't favourites" she said with amateurish logic.

"So what's your level stake to win 25 grand?"

"Three thousand" said Clarissa.

"Three grand!" echoed Baxter. "You can't afford to have any losers then!"

"But I told you William, I don't. My ex-husband is a difficult man but he's shrewd and he has told me in his own words that Bartenders Socks at Kelso is the business."

Again Baxter didn't know the animal. The

information seemed confined to poor horses in poor races – a recipe for disaster in Baxter's opinion. Clarissa ended by saying that she hoped they could meet up as soon as he was less busy.

Baxter refrained from putting up Bartenders Socks to his clients as it was in a field of six and looked like starting odds-on. However, he again backed it on the phone for 300 odd quid that was his returns from the Interesting Ant.

Backing winners was Baxter's consuming ambition but when Bartenders Socks dived up by 6 lengths, hard held, he felt strangely neutral. The price was 4 to 11 and it seemed to Baxter that backing at these prices was like juggling hand grenades – sooner or later one was going to go up in your face.

Over the next 10 days, Clarissa gave Baxter two more winners at prices of 2-7 and 4-9 making it four winners in a fortnight. Her ex-husband hadn't even trained these last two but clearly knew what was going on. Meanwhile, Baxter had allowed his winnings to accumulate and was now looking at having £800 on the next one.

Having begun with lukewarm enthusiasm for Clarissa's information, Baxter was becoming fascinated by just how long it would go on until the inevitable loser appeared. What he had overlooked, however, was the fulfilment of his part in the arrangement.

The next time Clarissa rang, the voice was still pleasant but assertive. "I need to see you, William."

"Still rather busy, I'm afraid" replied Baxter. "I thought you was ringing with some more information."

"I am, I'm informing you that I want to see you by this Friday or I shan't be talking to you again. It's all very well me passing on winning horses to you but what do I get out of it? I need a man, William. If you recall, I used the word 'vigorous' in the advert."

Baxter did recall the word and the reminder made him think and then gulp.

"Well?" said Clarissa, breaking the ensuing silence.

"Well, what?" replied Baxter with a little cough.

"I want you to take me out on Friday and I want no excuses. I'll give you my address and expect you to pick me up at seven."

"Any tips?" asked Baxter mildly.

"None whatsoever and nor will there be unless you keep this date! Don't worry William, I won't eat you!"

Baxter wasn't reassured - the woman sounded ravenous. He looked down at the address Clarissa had given him. D-day was arriving.

The days leading up to Friday, found Baxter worrying about a situation which he never expected to find himself in – that involving a woman. Indeed, he'd spent most of his adult life avoiding them.

He rooted out the original advert and read it again. 'Attractive, vivacious' Clarissa had described herself. Yes, well, it was all a matter of opinion, thought Baxter. All the husbands married to ugly women probably thought they were attractive, otherwise they wouldn't have married them. Then there was the matter of Baxter deciding quite how he fitted the description of 'vigorous, handsome and knows how to treat a woman.' He was clearly an impostor and all he could offer in defence was that he'd read the offer of racing information and forgotten everything else. Still, he decided, it was all a bit of a game. People misled each other with overblown opinions about themselves and were probably happy to settle for a lot less. The word 'vigorous' still bothered him, though.

When Friday arrived, Baxter decided he had to go. Good information, however useless it was to his business, still had some merit and he was keen on boosting his accrued winnings.

What made him nervous, though, was the possibility of having to spend a boring evening with some ghastly woman and he decided he needed an escape route.

He was contemplating this problem in the Drover's Arms at lunchtime when he noted the muscular, rugged barman and remembered he had a reputation as something of a Lothario. Baxter approached the bar and coughed to get the young man's attention.

"I'm sure you've been on a few blind dates before now" said Baxter.

"Certainly have" smiled the barman.

"Supposing you turned up to meet the other person and you immediately decided you didn't want to go through with it?"

"Easy" he said, the smile turning into a grin. "I'd suddenly start wheezing and tell her I'd have to cancel because I was having an asthma attack."

Baxter considered this for a moment and was

impressed for he reckoned even he could manage a bit of wheezing.

"That's brilliant!"

"It's an old trick but life's too short to dance with an ugly woman" were the barman's words of wisdom.

"Too right" agreed Baxter, although he had little experience of dancing with women of any description.

He was feeling a little less anxious about meeting the woman now but didn't feel up to going to Ascot as intended - besides which, he wouldn't have got back in time. Instead he spent the afternoon practising an asthmatic wheeze and reckoned he'd got it off to a tee by the time he started to get ready. He put on his best shirt and tie and a dark suit that needed a press but wasn't going to get one. Baxter appraised himself in the mirror and decided the reflection was not handsome but quite a bit better than it looked most days.

Outside he got a taxi and told the driver the address in Notting Hill. Sitting in the back he felt nervous, a feeling which slowly escalated to a state of panic. He felt like a grouse being beaten towards the guns. When the taxi stopped, his face was a lather of sweat and he'd had to undo the collar of his shirt and loosen his tie.

He told the taxi driver to wait and approached the door of a smart terraced house. Before pressing the bell, he took a deep breath, wiped his forehead with a hanky and reminded himself to wheeze if he needed to.

The door was opened by a woman in her 40's,

the sight of whom immediately made Baxter feel better. There was no need for an escape route for the woman was an absolute beauty even to the eye of Baxter. The pair looked at each other. Baxter smiled as the woman glanced him from head to toe. He was about to introduce himself when she suddenly touched her neck and said in a wheezing voice.

"I'm sorry I won't be able to come – I'm having an asthma attack!"

DIAMOND JACK

Mr Sprague was the manager of the bank unfortunate enough to hold Baxter's account, which swung between debit and credit with the volatility of a roller coaster carriage. This unsympathetic gentleman had studied the latest position and decided to derail it. The loan had been unserviced for several months, overdraft facilities had already been withdrawn and Baxter was now asked to return his chequebook and make immediate repayment of the loan. Indeed, the letter from Mr Sprague was so venomous that Baxter felt it should have been accompanied by a vaccine.

His current impecunious state was due to a volley of arrowed misfortunes that Fate had targeted at him. Apart from the usual run of bad luck which was a constant thorn in his side, Baxter had been hit by a rent increase from Mrs Wilbow, an expensive root treatment for one of his teeth and, the most damaging of all, a demand for £1500 from Inland Revenue.

Windsor was about as far as he could afford to travel, so it was here on a warm July evening that found him at the Berkshire course trying to redeem the situation.

It had never been a lucky course for Baxter and his fourth loser in a row underlined the fact. Baxter looked at the official photo-finish print and shook his head in dismay. The horse that beat Baxter's selection must have sneezed on the line - that's how close it was. He was absolutely on the floor. Any more of this, he concluded and he'd be between the joists.

Unusually dejected and worried, he made for the exit when he heard his name called. He turned around to see the grinning face of Diamond Jack who was holding a considerable wedge of tens and twenties in his hand.

"How's your luck?"

"Not as good as yours it seems" replied Baxter. "Where have you been?"

"Usual place, Scrubs this time. Been out since May" said Jack still flashing a smile. "Come and have a drink."

The whisky improved Baxter's demeanour and Jack was always amusing. For a born loser who was forever in and out of prison, he had a great appetite for life. He was called Diamond Jack because he specialised in diamonds of all sorts - cut, uncut, always stolen and often fake. Of course, pretending they weren't meant he offended certain people, particularly the police who had arranged several tours of Her Majesty's hotels for him.

"I'm on an unbelievable roll at the moment, Baxter" he said with relish. "I tell you, I borrowed two grand from an old biddy in Brighton and I've not looked back since."

"Someone lent you £2000?" said Baxter with incredulity.

"That's right, she's a do-gooder, a widow. The prison give me her address. She helps ex-cons when they come out."

"I could do with a loan myself" admitted Baxter. "I can't even get you a drink - I'm brasic at the moment."

"No problem" said Diamond Jack and ordered two more drinks. "Tell you what, why don't you go and see the old dear? Pretend you're an ex-con - she won't ask you for details. Mind you, two grand's her maximum and you're supposed to pay her back each month."

"Will it work?" asked Baxter, whose credit rating was such that any loan application he made had the same chance of success as a hedgehog crossing the M25.

"Look, she lent me the money and I've just come out after two years for deception - you're a cinch."

"What about these repayments - is there any interest?"

Diamond Jack spluttered into his glass. "Course there's no interest and, in my case, no repayments either. She's a million."

It all seemed too easy to Baxter's sharp mind.

"So where's her security?"

"Ah well, she's got this little Japanese fellow she calls her minder. I tell you, if he was in a fight with a hobgoblin, I'd back the hobgoblin. She hasn't got a clue." He pulled out a swollen wallet and handed Baxter a card and a £20 note. "Do yourself a favour - go and see her."

Before he could reply, Jack had left.

On the train back, Baxter checked the

presence of the card in his breast pocket and was re-assured. It was about time Windsor had brought him a bit of luck. Unfortunately, it hadn't.

By coincidence, there was racing at Brighton the next day, but Baxter had neither the money or the appetite to indulge it. He left a barren message on his racing line that 'there was no information worthy enough to pass on to his esteemed clients' but omitted to add that this had never stopped him before.

Outside Brighton station, it began to rain. Baxter looked at the card Diamond Jack had given him and for the first time he noticed that the name on it was 'Mrs P. Dockertee' - an unusual spelling. The name rang loudly in Baxter's memory because a J.Dockertee was the only bookmaker ever to have welshed on him. He'd been a third row bookmaker at several tracks in the south and had taken a chance on a fancied runner for the Victoria Cup, laying - it to lose 200 big ones. The horse had won and Dockertee should have been wiped out. Instead, he disappeared which meant that no one, including Baxter, got paid. Baxter had stubbornly kept his ante-post voucher although its prospect was about as good as a peace treaty signed by Atilla the Hun.

Anyway, he hoped the old lady was at home as it was hardly the weather for the beach.

"Is this place far?" inquired Baxter of a youngster practising wrestling holds with a mountain bike.

The boy looked at the card and gave Baxter directions. Having followed them for 20 minutes, he found himself back at the station feeling extremely disgruntled and considerably wetter. He presumed it had been his misfortune to ask the village idiot for directions. Having cast a vengeful eye for the boy, he got into a waiting taxi and shouted the address.

It was an imposing Georgian terraced house with a heavy doorknocker. Its dull thud produced a tiny oriental figure in a butler's outfit.

"I've come to see Mrs Dockertee" said Baxter.

"Come" was all the little man said.

Baxter was deciding whether to step over him or by him when a large over-dressed woman came down a stairway to the hall.

"Can I help you?" she said affectedly.

Baxter explained that Diamond Jack had recommended he come to see her. She nodded and he followed her into the lounge.

"And what did you think of Wormwood Scrubs then?" she asked.

"Er, well, you know how it is" mumbled Baxter, not meaning to allot a criminal record to the woman but feeling increasingly uncomfortable with the situation.

Mrs Dockertee disregarded the remark and spoke about kindness being the best rehabilitation for criminals and how privileged she was to be able to help. While she prattled on with her good intentions and worthiness, Baxter's eyes wandered about the room until a face from the past stared back at him from a large photo over the mantelpiece. Baxter inched forward involuntary to smack his fist into the offending features for they were those of Jim Dockertee.

Baxter interrupted the flow. "Is that your husband?" he asked sharply.

"A tiny oriental figure in a butler's outfit"

"He was - I'm a widow. Fortunately, he left me well provided for so I'm able to do my social work and employ the services of my helper, Danyo."

The abbreviated butler must have been standing behind a table leg because he suddenly appeared and bowed to the old lady.

Baxter's unease was growing.

"Well then" he smacked his hands together to release the tension "if you can let me have the money, I'll be off - £2000 will be great."

She nodded towards Danyo, who gave Baxter a plastic envelope containing £50 notes.

"I'm not a charity, so it's a loan and not a gift. There's a note inside giving you instructions about the monthly repayments. Danyo here is very strict in this regard, you see honour is very important to him and he is devoted to me."

Baxter smiled and thanked the widow. Being able to get away and with the money in his pocket, Baxter was feeling considerably better. Danyo opened the door for him and Baxter ruffled the sleek black hair as he left.

"Goodbye, little fellow" he said.

The next moment, Baxter was circling the air like an ignited Catherine wheel before spluttering out and landing flat on his back. At first, he thought the Japanese midget had done it but when he looked up Mrs Dockertee was standing besides her butler.

"You must be careful, Mr Baxter, you just tripped on the step."

Despite his fall, Baxter knew he was himself again when he wondered if he could still make the last race at Brighton. His watch told him he couldn't so he bought a paper, found a pub and spent a pleasant hour studying tomorrow's card. The £2000 in his pocket was sending out a comforting message to Baxter. It said "You're back in business."

Of course, the Inland Revenue had to be paid, the bank could be mollified with a partial payment and Mrs Wilbow could wait because she always did.

Soon, the only note left in the packet was the one regarding repayments.

Baxter's response was to send a scribbled letter explaining how Jim Dockertee had welshed on the ante-post bet and that with interest on the unpaid money, the £2000 his widow had given him just about sufficed. He also enclosed the voucher for the bet.

The following couple of months were quite good for Baxter. His stable contacts were coming up with some nice winners and his racing adverts, while not hysterical, did have something to shout about for a change. The bank had now been appeased and Mr Sprague had earlier given him an acknowledgment in the street although, as Baxter was coming out of Armstrong's betting shop, it had a certain misgiving.

Baxter looked up to see Mrs Wilbow at his door.

"You've not come to ask for the rent again, Mrs Wilbow?"

"Well, I would if I thought I'd get it" she reproved him. "No, there's a little man outside wants to see you."

"Little man" repeated Baxter. He was

encouraged by the description whereas 'big' would have been a cause for concern. "Not a jockey, is he?"

"I don't know, he's not sitting on a horse" replied Mrs Wilbow.

Reminded that, in the wrong mood, Mrs Wilbow was not averse to a bit of irony, Baxter asked the landlady to send the man up.

If anything, Danyo looked even smaller than before.

"You remember me?" he said. "Letter for you."

"Of course, I do." Baxter got up and walked across to take the letter.

Danyo watched him closely as he read it. *'Dear Mr Baxter, you have broken the terms of the loan. The follow-up to default in repayments is a visit by my representative, Danyo, and I strongly advise that you pay him the arrears of £200 immediately. Your earlier letter regarding a business deal with my late husband is something I know nothing about and quite irrelevant to the matter of the loan. Yours sincerely, Mrs P. Dockertee.'*

"Irrelevant, is it!" said Baxter, screwing up the page and tossing it on the floor.

"You don't pay?" asked Danyo

"Too right I don't pay" said Baxter taking an aggressive stance and reckoning the worst the dehydrated dwarf could do was to pommel his kneecaps.

"That bad for you" were the last words Baxter heard before a darkness descended upon him. Mrs Wilbow reported that she heard a lot of banging and falling about. The paramedics reported that it was the worst case they'd seen since a farmer walked into a threshing machine.

When he eventually came around, Baxter ached from head to toe with his body bound either by bandages or plaster of Paris and supported by slings and pulleys. In his mind, he traced the pain back to its source and the vision of the pocket psychopath appeared.

He panicked and called out to whoever was in earshot.

"Help me! I need to borrow £200. This is urgent! Is anyone listening?"

The person in the next bed was also constricted by a mass of bandages but he called back through heavily swollen lips.

"Hello Baxter, I've sort of been expecting you."

It was Diamond Jack.

THE PURRFECT GIFT

Baxter was in a febrile mood. He looked anxiously at the phone on his desk, waiting to snatch it up the moment it rang. It remained stubbornly silent. He got up and cast a glance at the clock hands on the face of Lester Piggott. The SureFire Tipping Service was supposed to be on line at 10 a.m. It was 9.50 and he was waiting for a call from his contact in Middleham. The stable was in blistering form and Baxter was reaping the reward as new subscribers to his tipping line came in at an unprecedented rate. Baxter had been in the game long enough to know that it couldn't last and had been getting stuck into the information with such zeal that his was almost ripping the stitching from bookmaker's satchels. He grabbed the phone and listened to check he was still connected.

Reassured, he started to pace the room but found his movement restricted by the sheer clutter in the room which was a cross between an assault course and a junk shop. Mrs Wilbow had long refused to clean it. She was right to do so for had she ventured into such chaos, she would likely have disappeared and been pronounced 'missing - presumed lost'.

His first step found a disregarded rich tea finger, his second the cap of a pen which snapped in protest and the third, the pen itself which took on the action of a roller-skate. The resultant impromptu gymnastics gave him a nasty turn and resolved him to return to the sanctuary of his chair. He poured himself a coffee and was suddenly aware of being watched. A scrawny black and white cat was sat up on a pile of telephone directories and regarded him calmly.

"Where the hell did you come from?" said Baxter aloud.

The phone rang - Baxter snatched it up.

"Yes, the form's good" Baxter put in as if to confirm the blandishments at the other end. "Win a minute will it? Okay. Thanks. Must go!" He slammed down the phone and hurried to get the golden information on line.

He'd forgotten about the cat until his cup of coffee fell over and spilled onto his desk. The feline made no apologies and even paddled in the liquid while Baxter scrambled to evade the brown waterfall trickling onto his trousers. He grabbed a cloth.

"Stupid cat!" remarked Baxter, patting the pools in an undomesticated way. "You can shove off!"

The cat stared back blankly at him and, without protest, allowed Baxter to deposit it on the ledge of the open window from which it had come.

Baxter checked his keys, money, racing paper and binoculars and was off to King's Cross to catch the train for York. A final glance around the office showed the cat had re-entered and was settling down in an old shoe-box on the filing cabinet. Baxter gave a wry smile and closed the door.

It was then that an odd sequence of events conspired to prevent him getting to York. First of all, a passenger on the bus Baxter was travelling on was taken ill. The bus was stopped, an ambulance was called and a seat was propped against the rear of the bus. Baxter got up and cast a diagnostic eye over the collapsed figure.

"He doesn't look too bad to me" he said, patently ignoring the grey hue of the man's face. "Could we at least push on to King's Cross"?

The driver to whom this question was addressed gave Baxter such a repugnant look that he decided to get off before hearing the reply. He hailed a taxi and had gone no more than half a mile when it collided with a lorry. Baxter was unhurt but before he knew it, the police arrived and detained him as a witness despite his protest that he would miss his train. A second taxi got him there with minutes to spare. He rushed to the booking window and asked for a ticket to York. The man gave a long glance at Baxter, walked away and came back after an inordinately long time.

"Bad news I'm afraid, sir - this is a forgery."

"What!" replied Baxter, already highly agitated by his wait.

"Could you come with me, sir?" said a voice behind him.

After some difficult questioning by the Transport Police, Baxter was released. He now resigned himself to the fact that he had not only missed his train but that his winnings from Lingfield the previous day had contained a dud £50 note.

The saloon bar of the Drover's Arms was a haven after all the hassle. He ordered a whisky with his lunch and sank himself into his racing paper.

"The feline paddled in the liquid"

Baxter felt enormously refreshed when he entered Armstrong's shop but not quite enough to offer any repartee to the comment "Bit overdressed ain't you mate? It's only a betting shop."

However, he removed the bins from around his neck, took off his trilby and put one inside the other.

"Hello, Baxter" called Armstrong from behind the counter "how's your luck?"

"Very good" admitted Baxter. "And yours?"

"The results are brilliant. We're winning well lately."

"I'll have to ask for a rise then" smiled Doris, an attractive blonde cashier who wore very short skirts for a woman in her 40's. "Here" she handed Baxter a plastic bag "put those in here - you'll ruin your hat."

Baxter restored the hat to his head and put the bins in the bag.

"I've got one today" he said quietly to Armstrong. "Ouch Couture, in the first at York - it'll probably win."

The bookmaker looked at his sheet.

"At 6 to 4 it probably won't" he said with mathematical reasoning. You can have it for as much as you like - that's what I'm here for. Anyway, it's got a bad draw and the jockey's a clown."

Armstrong's cockiness had slightly undermined Baxter's confidence so that when the show came up, he only had £200 at 6 to 4. When it drifted to 2 to 1 he was going to top up but as he contemplated they were suddenly off. It was a good race, on the nod but Ouch Couture was beaten a sneeze.

Baxter signalled his departure to Doris and managed to smile.

Armstrong called out.

"Told you, I'm unbeatable at the moment - thanks for dropping in."

Baxter stopped at the supermarket on the way back and for some unaccountable reason found himself basketing a couple of tins of cat food with his bottle of whisky. He didn't even like cats much, he thought as he climbed the stairs. Horses were great, especially ones who stuck their head out in front at the sign of the lollipop. Dogs, too, he liked but cats left him quite neutral.

Inside his office, the cat was noisily appreciating the plate of cat food while Baxter sipped his whisky. Not a good day, he reflected. Perhaps his winning run had come to an end, he wondered. Indeed, it had and with a vengeance.

The chronicling of the misfortunes that befell Baxter and the SureFire Tipping Service would have had a tragedian's pen bouncing happily across the page. The information that had been red-hot went so cold it might have come from Pluto.

Fifteen consecutive losers were served to his subscribers so culling all but the most masochistic who presumably thought it just preferable to slashing their wrists.

But it hadn't stopped there. Several cheques had bounced from previously honourable clients, his Lester Piggott clock had packed it in and when his electric kettle exploded like an atomic bomb, the shock caused him to slip and break his ankle. Finally Mrs Wilbow's local bingo hall had shut prompting the deprived landlady to demand some instant money so she could cheer herself up.

The cat, however, was doing fine and appeared unaware of the increasing doubtful glances from Baxter. Like most gamblers, Baxter was superstitious so that at various times he'd had lucky socks, lucky ties and lucky pens. He'd even had a lucky rich tea finger until he ate it by mistake and was surprised that such a charmed biscuit could taste so awful even if it had been a month old. Likewise, bad luck also had to be identified and avoided. There were certain bookmakers Baxter refused to bet with and his wardrobe was devoid of anything coloured green. This time, despite his reluctance, he kept coming round to the cat. Things had certainly gone pear-shaped since its arrival. The entrance of Mrs Wilbow interrupted this conviction.

"You look different, Mrs Wilbow" he said with a puzzled gaze.

"I should do, this lot cost me the twenty five pounds I squeezed out of you" she said touching her hair. Baxter's expression indicated that he didn't consider his cash well-spent. "Anyway, I've got the answer to the bad luck you keep complaining about" she went on. "Feng-shui is what you need." Before Baxter could reply she was off again. "I was reading this article under the hair-dryer. What you have to do is harness the heavens and earth to bring health and good fortune."

"And this bloke can do this?" asked Baxter derisively.

"Feng-shui is not a bloke - it's from China. It means arranging your furniture in certain groupings" she said with disdain. "I thought you would have known that. She put the magazine down on his desk. "They said I could borrow it to show you. I reckon it's what you need."

His landlady then turned and left.

Baxter thought the whole thing a load of nonsense but it had one redeeming factor. Since his enforced stay in hospital, he'd developed a healthy respect for anything oriental. In fact, it was a healthy respect born out of ill-health as he still got the occasional twinge in his neck.

Having read about positive ch'i, 'secret arrows' and Pa Kua mirrors, he still thought it a load of nonsense. However, he was desperate for a change in his fortunes and if it worked he didn't care. He looked for a Feng-shui practitioner in Yellow Pages - there was only one.

"You want me to design your head office, is that right?" said Mr Taikoo.

"Well, yes" said Baxter, thinking the statement a bit overdone but unable to fault it in essence.

Mr Taikoo took down the address. "I don't know the building - are you near the High Street?"

"Quite near" said Baxter vaguely.

At 11 o'clock precisely Mr Taikoo arrived. He was immaculately suited and overpoweringly scented with his oriental features creased by a wide smile and topped by ebony plastered-down hair.

He shook hands.

"Shall we talk on the way to your offices - I have another appointment at twelve?"

"This is the office" replied Baxter.

"What! You mean this......this" he waved his hands around the mish mash of objects and debris "is what you consulted me about?"

"Yes" said Baxter "I thought you could make a few changes. As long as it doesn't cost more than a fifty."

The figure of Mr Taikoo was now hopping around like a barefooted man who has just stepped on an electric plug. He was still howling with rage as he descended the stairs.

"Nothing inscrutable about him" thought Baxter.

The next day, a conclusion was reached. The cat was a *boch* and had to go before Baxter fell under a bus or was reduced to selling copies of Big Issue. He had some sympathy for the cat, however, and realised he couldn't just abandon the animal he had unwittingly adopted. The problem was solved that afternoon when he attended Armstrong's betting shop.

Baxter's broken ankle meant that he couldn't go racing for the time being so he now idled around in Armstrong's shop watching the T.V. screens and trying to spot future winners. It was the commentary of the second race at Redcar that was interrupted by a feminine scream as a mouse scuttled across the floor showing more speed than the horse written on Baxter's betting slip.

"If you don't get the rat-catcher from the

council down here, I'm leaving" said Doris.

"It's harmless" said Armstong.

"It scares me and besides, it's a health hazard" insisted Doris, wriggling on her stool and showing more leg than ever. "It runs around like it owns the place."

Baxter felt a little crafty when he said to Doris.

"I've got a cat you can have - that'll solve your problem."

"Oh-h I like cats" said Doris.

"I don't know about that" said Armstrong overhearing.

He was too late. Even with his broken ankle, Baxter was out the door.

Baxter's limp made it an uneven carriage for the cat but its arrival at the shop was greeted warmly by Doris and less so by Armstrong. Off-loading the cat was like backing a winner to Baxter so he pressed his luck, had a £1 yankee and left before the cat could be returned to him.

Checking the results later, he discovered he'd backed another four winners because the yankee had come up.

Presenting his ticket the next day, Baxter commented "Bit of luck that."

"Yes," said Armstrong "we had our first losing day for weeks yesterday."

At the back of the shop, Doris was putting some food out for the cat.

Baxter stayed long enough to watch his tipping line selection romp home and this time placed a £2 yankee before leaving. Incredibly, they too all won. Baxter had definitely cracked it!

There was quite a queue around the pay-out in Armsrong's shop the next day and Baxter was offered a cheque instead of cash.

"Everyone's winning" explained Armstrong "I can't understand it - I'm getting absolutely slaughtered."

Baxter accepted a cheque for £756 and placed it in his wallet.

Armstong was almost confidential.

"That cat......." he said to Baxter.

"Don't you blame the cat" cut in Doris. "Anyway it's got rid of the mice."

"No" said Armstrong apologetically "I just wondered if you found the cat unlucky?"

"Well, personally, I'm not superstitious in that respect" lied Baxter "and I'm surprised that you are. You know it's a load of nonsense."

"I suppose so" said Armstrong dismally and took the £3 yankee that a smiling Baxter handed him and which Baxter just knew was probably going to win.

TALKING THE HORSE

Shakespeare was an out and out punter, decided Baxter. Why else would he have written the line "the slings and arrows of outrageous fortune"? In fact, Baxter reckoned the Bard of Stratford had probably penned it after doing his brains at a Southwark cock-fight and then, in trying to get out of trouble, had plunged on the favourite in the tilt festival only to see him stab his lance into the ground and thus inadvertently introduce pole-vaulting as a sport. Four hundred years later, Baxter was feeling the same hopelessness and suffering as the old pen-pusher for the missiles were finding him an easy target.

The wounds were such that Baxter had arranged an interview with his bank manager. The interview was brief and unsatisfactory for Mr Sprague not only refused to extend the existing overdraft facilities but also muted their imminent closure.

The effort required to attend the interview at the early hour of 9.30 a.m. had deserved a better fate, reflected Baxter, although, in truth, the manager had been true to form. Like all non-racing men, there was no sympathy for 157's, short head defeats, diabolical disqualification and Machiavellian trainers. Baxter could also have mentioned his ante-post good thing that needed good ground and, the day before the race, Newmarket got more wet stuff than an

Amazon rain forest.

Of course, the sight of the 'Racing Post' projecting from his raincoat pocket had not helped his cause and had merely tightened the tap of Mr Sprague's charity that even in full flow would not have exceeded a trickle. Baxter, though, would not have understood such prejudice for he believed everyone should share his fondness for racing. A pageant of expectation played out against a backdrop of intriguing characters and wonderful racecourses. He took the journal from his pocket and, unfolding it as he went along, began to read with half an eye on the road ahead.

As he approached the downstairs entrance to his office, the enormous tote dividend for the winner of the 2.15 Bangor caught his attention so that he vaguely took the key from his pocket and pushed it into the lock. The door, already being ajar, opened up effortlessly and surprised Baxter. His second surprise was to see Mrs Wilbow bent over an ugly potted plant, which had received a goodly number of fag ends from Baxter over the years.

"Good morning, my little precious, how are you today? I hope you're feeling better because you've not looked very well lately."

This was Mrs Wilbow addressing the plant.

Because of the broom leaning across the hallway, Baxter was unable to squeeze by as he would have liked. He coughed.

"Morning, Mrs Wilbow."

His landlady turned around.

"I didn't hear you" she said. "You just caught

me talking to my plant."

Baxter tried not to look too alarmed at what he regarded as early signs of mental disorder.

"You must have heard about it" she went on. "They say if you talk kindly and caringly to plants, they respond and grow better."

Baxter hadn't heard about it at all and was extremely glad that the 'Racing Post' had not squandered valuable space on such piffle.

"It works too, you know" she continued. "That one in my window box has come on lovely since I've been doing it."

Baxter smiled sympathetically. The 'plant' to which she referred was in fact a weed masquerading as whatever she thought it was. He climbed the stairs with the optimistic thought that if Mrs Wilbow's addling of the brain continued it might affect her memory of his overdue rent.

Closing the office door was like raising the drawbridge to his castle - a private stronghold where horseracing was paramount and strategy in the ceaseless battle to beat the bookies was planned. To reach the desk and chair by the window, it was necessary to negotiate several hurdles in the form of old 'Racing Posts', even older 'Sporting Lifes', racing magazines and cardboard boxes. As a course specialist, Baxter made it look easy.

A miscellany of papers was cleared from the desk by stuffing them into a drawer revealing a phone, a large ash-tray and a half-eaten sandwich. To one side was a trolley holding an electric kettle and his coffee-time kit. He switched on the kettle, put the coffee in the cup and looked around the enclosure.

A filing cabinet, fat with papers spilling out from every drawer stood beneath a wall-clock in the shape of Lester Piggott's face. On various parts of the floor were a jockey's whip, racing photos, Ruff's Guides, Raceforms, bank statements, a print of Mill Reef with the picture cord broken, a sprinkling of once valued but now abandoned ante-post vouchers, an umbrella and a pair of socks. The kettle steamed, Baxter made his coffee, sat down, lit a cigarette and spread his paper fondly before him. It was the best part of the day. Hope abounded, the prize of great rewards was there to be taken. For the moment, at least, Life was good.

By the time of the last race that afternoon, it had deteriorated greatly. The nap of the day, which he had given so confidently to the subscribers of his SureFire Tipping Service, had appeared to run with a limp and its mentor anticipated a further spate of abusive mail.

The racing had been on television that day, which was fortunate as Baxter couldn't afford to travel to Chester. However, apart from the irritation of seeing his selections beat, Baxter had been rather prickled at the lack of information given about a character seen in the parade ring before each race. On each occasion he could be seen talking animatedly to one horse just prior to the jockey mounting and, even more remarkably, each horse had won.

Clearly not an owner or trainer by his manner and dress, the TV commentators had never mentioned the man. Instead they interviewed a jockey 'who was a bit unlucky' but who, in fact, had ridden a stinker and a trainer – his horse backed off the boards in a massacre of the bookies – who had the audacity to say the win was 'quite unexpected'. Of the horse-talker, though, there was only mystery.

Baxter lit a cigarette and pondered. Deep in thought, he was suddenly distracted by the scraping sound of a broom on the stairs and Mrs Wilbow's version of 'If I Ruled the World'. The rating of their discord, Baxter adjudged to be a dead-heat but it also reminded him about Mrs Wilbow and her plants.

After further thought, he decided the plants theory was definitely nonsense and only suitable for those seeking achievement in outstanding stupidity. However, he was not so anxious to exclude the possibility of horse talk and rather liked the idea of communicating with horses. Indeed, he could recall countless occasions when the horse language equivalent of 'you couldn't beat my Pekinese', 'where's your cart?' and 'four-legged bandit' would have been very convenient. Yes, Baxter assured himself, if horses had ears and made noises it was a reasonable assumption that they were able to communicate. It also seemed that this mystery man had cracked the code.

The following morning, Baxter was intrigued by the advert in the 'Racing Post'. It said simply 'The sensational Prof. Higgins will be available to trainers and owners at Haydock Park today'. Now, Baxter's knowledge of books and films was scant to say the least but he did seem to remember hearing the name before. His memory was jogged and slowly the rather faded pictures came back to him.

He had taken a rare excursion to the cinema

with a decidedly ugly woman who, it was said, had a brother in a Newmarket stable. Ever seeking new contacts, at whatever discomfort, Baxter had paid good money for two front stall seats of "My Fair Lady" and witnessed a Professor Higgins speaking a song called 'Talk to the Animals'. The evening had been totally unrewarding when he discovered that the brother worked not in a racing stable but in a riding stable. The woman had been swiftly dispatched and only now did it seem something worthwhile could arise from the experience.

Baxter assumed that the horse talker on TV and the man advertising himself as Professor Higgins were one and the same. This was confirmed when he recognised the man leaning on the paddock fence just before the first race at Haydock Park. The man looked a bit of a rustic with a red hue to his face, a flat tweed cap, long raincoat and trousers tucked into knee-length wellington boots.

"Professor Higgins" said Baxter.

The man turned around eagerly but seeing Baxter, his eyes narrowed.

"You don't look like an owner or trainer and you not be a horse and them's the only ones I talk to at races."

Baxter tried to look appealing.

"Look, I saw you on the tele yesterday – amazing! Every horse you spoke to won. How about a tip for today?"

"Nothing this race – not been engaged" said the professor tersely. He ended with a wink that rather confused Baxter.

"He recognised the man leaning on the paddock fence"

With the professor not involved, Baxter let the first race pass. However, his hopes rose when he returned to the paddock for the second race for standing in the centre was the professor and one of the few trainers Baxter believed had not earned himself a prison sentence. It looked as though a horse called Killer Egg was to get the Higgins treatment and was certainly one with a good chance according to Baxter.

As the horse was lead in to be mounted, Baxter watched the professor grasp the reins and pull the head towards him. He then proceeded to give it a short verbal indoctrination which pinned back the horse's ears and sent Baxter off to find a bookmaker he could pulverise. Killer Egg's price was shortening like snapped elastic. Baxter missed 5's, had a good bet at 4's and topped up with a bit of 7-2.

They were off as Baxter hurried away to watch the race from the stands. After four furlongs of the mile race, Baxter had his binoculars firmly fixed on Killer Egg and felt a familiar horrid feeling engulfing him. Killer Egg was already being scrubbed along with little response and at the distance was out with the washing. Baxter was angry, strangled his tickets before stamping on them, and sought out Professor Higgins for some abuse.

He found him at the bottom of the steps.

"Communication problem was there?" asked Baxter scornfully. "I thought the horses were supposed to win when you spoke to them."

The professor looked offended.

"Only if I tell them to" he said. "The animal was told not to exert itself, to simply have an easy gallop. These instructions I received from his owner, Mr Hayward."

Baxter winced and recalled the name on his discarded betting tickets.

"Jack Hayward, the bookie?" wailed Baxter.

"Not sure of his business" said the professor. "You can just see him over there standing on a box. The man with a big smile on his face."

UNSUITED BY BRIGHTON

Baxter got up and, having washed and shaved, approached his wardrobe. Dressed only in underwear, it was not an elegant figure and even the addition of outer vestments only improved it slightly for Baxter's range of clothes was both minimal and dated.

Baxter excused this sartorial deficiency on the grounds that he was too busy to go shopping for new clothes although, of course, lack of funds didn't help. In fact, he did like to look smart occasionally and his ambition was that one day he would be completely outfitted by Herbie Frogg of Jermyn Street. So far, though, his only affordable purchase from that establishment was a tie.

He eyed the rail of clothes with a studied look. Normally, the choice of what to wear was haphazard and given little thought but today he was going to a funeral and was deciding on his best suit. This was a bit like picking the least discredited in a small field of selling platers. However, having to be of a dark material the choice was reduced to two and then quickly to no choice when he discovered that one had bell-bottom trousers. How he'd kept them all this time, he couldn't imagine. He could only assume they'd been lucky at some stage and as he'd survived his youth without getting married perhaps he'd kept it out of gratitude. He hung the suit back in the wardrobe and put on the only remaining selection.

It was locating his black tie that took so long. He finally discovered it lodged behind a radiator, showing several stains and a greasy surface sheen. The item needed replacing for Baxter could foresee the increasing use of a black tie as he got older. Indeed, Victor Blake was only 52 and here was Baxter getting ready for the man's funeral.

There was a steady rain falling as Baxter approached his office. After leaving his usual on-line message of hope for the faithful but foolish, he closed the door of the SureFire Tipping Service and went to look for a taxi. It would have been easier to use the mini-cab office a couple of doors away but he wanted to arrive at the cemetery in a style superior to his clothes.

There was a largish crowd at the cemetery for Victor Blake was a popular racing figure. The bookmaker had suffered a heart attack at Newbury during a ding-dong struggle up the straight between the favourite and a 20-1 shot. It seemed that the strain had all been a bit too much for Victor but as the outsider got up in a photo, it was agreed that he hadn't died in vain.

Among the mourners was a tall, lean, man impeccably dressed and wearing a black bowler. Although he didn't know him personally, Baxter didn't like Galbraith. But then he never liked any trainer whose form reading of their horses was tricky to say the least. Galbraith especially, seemed to produce horses with form lines of more coconuts than a Caribbean greengrocer before sluicing in as an unlikely but well-backed winner.

The man had previously been a chemist which Baxter deemed a less than ideal background for getting a trainer's licence. Such was the unpredictability of Galbraith's horses that Baxter gave his runners and their races a wide berth. There was no doubt that the ex-chemist could train horses, it was just that their erratic running was a form student's nightmare. Baxter aired his frustration by referring to any Galbraith winner as 'one from the laboratory' although, it has to be said, without any justification.

After the chapel service, Baxter was in no particular hurry as the only meeting that day was at Kelso, a course too late to reach even if he had wanted to. He fell in step with a racing journalist and they went to a nearby pub.

"Know anything?" said the man bluntly.

"Not a thing at the moment - but I'd like to."

"Don't know how you survive, Baxter. Even the supply of mugs must dry up sooner or later."

"I've lived better" conceded Baxter, ignoring the aspersion. "What about you? I saw you talking to Galbraith."

"Yes, he said his Political Oxygen is a certainty at Brighton tomorrow. I'm not to tip it in my column though."

Baxter savoured his whisky. "Trouble is, Galbraith is a bit slippery. The man could escape from a strait-jacket without leaving a crease."

"I know what you're saying but he's never told me anything before. The horse is also entered up at Brighton on the Wednesday. Galbraith reckons he'll probably go in again. Loves to get his toe in and can't have it soft enough apparently so this rain's ideal. And don't go tipping it yourself. Any hint of money for one of his and the price disappears faster than togas at a Roman orgy.

The following day, it was raining again. Baxter had decided not to go to for a whiff of sea air but the race at Brighton was very much on his mind. He'd read the form of Political Oxygen and while it was extremely modest, it didn't seem to matter where Galbraith was concerned. Baxter was on the phone to his bookmaker shortly before the opening show of the 3 o'clock race at Brighton. It was a five furlongs sprint and Political Oxygen was amongst the bar prices. Moments later, Political Oxygen was 12's. Baxter stepped in with a £100 and took the 12-1. The returned starting price was 5-1 so there was clearly a few quid for the winner. Galbraith had struck again.

Wednesday was supposed to be the second day of the Brighton meeting but grey clouds were simply chucking it down and an inspection was due at mid-day. All the other scheduled meetings were off and so Baxter made one of his impulsive decisions. He would fulfil his ambition of being outfitted by Herbie Frogg. Why not? His winnings from Political Oxygen would be in his bank, racing looked like being off and he had no need to worry about a selection for his clients.

He drew the cash from his bank, and feeling particularly buoyant took a cab to Jermyn Street where he arrived about mid-day with the rain still falling heavily. On entering the shop, he was approached by a smiling man who quickly appraised Baxter's clothes and decided his offer of "May I be of assistance, sir?"

was like asking a drowning man whether he could do with a life-belt.

"Yes, I'd like a complete outfit from you. You know, shirt, tie, suit and socks."

"And shoes, sir?"

Baxter hadn't considered shoes although with size 12 feet it wasn't an easy oversight to make.

"Why not!" enthused Baxter.

The assistant thought they should begin with the suit and after selecting a bold brown check, the necessary process of measuring began. Another man ran a tape measure over Baxter's less than vital statistics and called them out to the assistant to write down. Baxter was rather enjoying being fussed over when suddenly another young man entered the shop wiping the rain from his face.

"Would you believe it – Brighton's only on!" he said aloud.

In fact, Baxter couldn't believe it but he remembered Political Oxygen was down to run in the first race and he intended to back it.

"Excuse me" said Baxter removing the tape measure from his person. He looked at his watch. "I've got to go. Hold everything. I'll be back very soon."

The two men hovering around Baxter looked pained. He grabbed his jacket and addressed the youngster.

"Thank goodness you're a racing man – where's the nearest betting shop?"

The shop in the Haymarket was rather noisy and full. The runners for the first race were parading

Unsuited by Brighton

"May I be of assistance, sir?"

and while several horses had been pulled out of the race, Baxter was delighted to see Political Oxygen was still a runner. He was deciding whether to take the show of even money when he was staggered to see the tall figure of Galbraith at the counter and pushing a lot of cash towards the clerk.

Baxter was a couple of places back in the queue but as Galbraith turned around, Baxter introduced himself.

"I saw you at Victor's funeral on Monday – thought you'd be at Brighton today."

Galbraith smiled thinly. "No, I've taken the day off. I'm doing a bit of shopping."

"Me, too" said Baxter. "Getting a suit and stuff at Herbie Frogg's. This is one of his ties." He lifted the tie for inspection.

"Really" replied Galbraith a little more warmly "I'm a Hermes man myself."

"Good thing this one of yours after the way it won here yesterday, isn't it?" asked Baxter.

"Well, he does have a penalty but he should run well." The trainer moved off.

Typical trainer, thought Baxter, never gives anything away. Anyway, penalty or not, he'd obviously backed it and if Political Oxygen liked to get his toe in, this amount of rain should ensure he'd get in his pastern and a bit of fetlock as well.

The brief conversation with Galbraith meant that he'd forgotten to take the price about Political Oxygen which was just as well for the manager would have undoubtedly only have laid him the price for £200 maximum and the horse had now gone to 5-4.

This apparent good fortune suddenly seemed uncertain and the sound of alarm bells rang in Baxter's mind as the horse now drifted out to 2-1 and there was a lot of support for a horse named Prince Pepper.

Baxter was wishing he'd cut back his bet of a long one. He looked around for Galbraith for some reassurance but couldn't see him. Baxter's misgivings were well-founded for Political Oxygen set off like his tail was on fire, petered right out in the last furlong and finished well-beaten behind the gambled-on Prince Pepper.

Baxter was well used to losing heavily but it still hurt. He sat down and lit a cigarette. Perhaps he was never meant to get outfitted by Herbie Frogg after all. Anyway, Galbraith had presumably done his money as well and if he'd got it wrong what chance did mere mortals like himself have?

It was shortly after the weighed-in announcement and Baxter was about to leave when the shop door opened and Galbraith entered putting away a mobile phone. The trainer went straight up to the counter and handed in a betting slip. The manager got up and came across to him.

"We wouldn't normally have this amount of cash in the shop but fortunately we took a large amount on something else in the race so it's okay."

"Glad to hear it" said Galbraith as he scooped up the notes.

As he turned around Baxter was facing him.

"You put me away, didn't you?"

"Not at all. I didn't say I'd backed my horse. You made an assumption" replied the trainer.

Baxter could only feel an over-riding sense of scorn.

"What d'you stop it with – something from your chemist's shop at home?"

"You're far too fanciful you know" smiled Galbraith. "It's possible my head lad may have given it a good drink of water – inadvertently, of course." He side-stepped Baxter and was gone.

The assistants in Herbie Frogg's were surprised and relieved at Baxter's reappearance.

"Ah, welcome back, sir" said one, picking up the tape again "I just need to take a few more measurements."

"You can forget all that. I shan't be buying a suit and all that other guff" said Baxter.

The assistant received this news with the disappointment of an Italian motorist who finds his horn doesn't work.

"Oh dear" he said and sat down with his unsmiling colleagues so that they were huddled together like shipwreck victims.

"What I have come back for though is a tie" said Baxter.

"A tie!" said the youngster with some derision.

One of the others got up and showed Baxter a rack holding a mass of colourful and brilliant designs. Baxter cast a covetous eye over them before saying.

"D'you happen to have a black tie?"

"A black tie?" echoed the assistant.

"Yes, you see, not only am I in mourning for a thousand pounds that passed away earlier but I do actually need one."

INFORMATION TO BOOT

The SureFire Tipping Service was having a disastrous run of late and the proprietor reviewed its recent performance as being more like the spluttering of a damp squib. Baxter's expression, although suitably grim, was quite out of character for he was by nature, an optimist - a quality required in great abundance in his precarious occupation as a racehorse tipster.

However, this particular barren period had occurred when his finances had already been badly strained when a distant uncle had quite inconsiderately decided to snuff it. The natural expense Baxter had incurred was even more regretted when he learnt that the uncle had bequeathed him nothing more than a potted geranium.

Baxter arrived stealthily at his office at 10 o'clock and carefully pinned a notice to the door – 'Mr Baxter is unfortunately ill and will be away until further notice'. Although this was certainly a lie, it did contain a grain of truth for he certainly didn't feel too clever.

He locked the door behind him and picked up his morning mail. They were mostly bills, but two letters containing cheques brought some slight relief. They were from new subscribers to his tipping service and proved to Baxter that gullibility was still alive and well.

In fact, he was rather surprised that he had

been able to arrive at the office without suffering any physical damage to his person. He had quite expected one or two of his less understanding clients to be lying in wait for him. Just at that moment, there was a sharp knock at the door. Baxter felt stabbed by the cold steel of fear. "Couldn't they read?" he thought, and sat there uncomfortable and not daring to move.

"You there, Mr Baxter?" He recognised the voice of Mrs Wilbow who lived downstairs and from whom he rented his office. "What's this silly notice doing here?" she asked as he unlocked the door to let her in. Measures to protect one's life and limb were hardly silly, thought Baxter. However, he smiled pleasantly at her.

"Hello, Mrs Wilbow. The notice is intended for one or two people whom I expect to call and don't wish to see. You know, timewasters and troublemakers, that type of person."

"You just missed one of them" said Mrs Wilbow flatly.

Baxter considered this news extremely fortunate and wondered if this heralded the change of luck he so badly needed.

"Did he say what he wanted?" he asked innocently.

"He wanted you, Mr Baxter. He said he'd wring your neck if he got hold of you. Big chap he was, looked like a docker or navvy."

Baxter gulped uncomfortably at the imagined result of such an encounter.

"Some people are just bad losers, Mrs Wilbow. I mean, one cannot be right all the time."

"He said you couldn't tip yourself out of bed" relayed the landlady.

Baxter considered the remark and deemed it unsuitable as an unsolicited testimonial in his advertisements.

"Well, thank you Mrs Wilbow. Is that all?"

"What about my rent? It's been five weeks now" she asked, showing him an outstretched palm which she knew instinctively had very little chance of receiving any money into it.

"Ah, that Mrs Wilbow will be dealt with very soon. I am expecting, any moment now, certain information that will improve my finances at a stroke. Just you wait and see."

"I keep waiting Mr Baxter but so far there's no seeing" said Mrs Wilbow.

Baxter quickly turned round, grabbed the unwelcome potted geranium from the wastepaper bin and placed it in her still-outstretched palm with the words "A little gift for you."

Considering the abject state of the plant, Mrs Wilbow seemed rather pleased so before she could speak, he manoeuvered her outside the office, relocked the door and sat down. It was a temporary respite but a more permanent improvement needed to be found. Unlike some tipsters, Baxter did, in fact, have some very good connections. It was just that these normally shrewd judges were coming unstuck. "One certain winner, just one. That's all I want" pleaded Baxter, trying to sound as undemanding as possible to the superior being he hoped might be listening and perhaps a racing man himself.

During these dismal times, Baxter regarded the racing papers with great scepticism. Any prolonged period without winners convinced him that skullduggery between trainers, jockeys, bookmakers, or even all three, was implicit. With these unkind thoughts, he looked at the first race of only six runners and tried to read the nefarious minds of the jockeys and trainers concerned in it. Having drawn up every combination of deceit and manipulation, he ended up with an awful headache and threw the paper down in disgust. It was at this moment that his eyes alighted on a small envelope that was tucked up near the corner of the door. Baxter wondered what sort of letter it was that he'd overlooked and picked it up. The words 'The Tippster' were scrawled across the envelope which was liberally punctuated with traces of a red sticky substance strongly resembling strawberry jam.

The writing inside was barely legible and was made even more difficult by atrocious spelling and further traces of the scribbler's diet. Eventually, Baxter discerned the general directive was for him to be at 'The Fryer Tuk Caff' where the writer would have some 'informashun' for him. Baxter's benevolence inclined him to think that the writer's information couldn't be worse than his grammar. He looked at his watch, grabbed his trilby and arrived at the rendezvous just on twelve.

A small pimply-faced boy was waiting outside and approached him.

"You the tipster?" he grinned cheekily.

Baxter, rather surprised and not liking small boys, especially pimply ones, admitted with some embarrassment that he was.

"And are you the person who writes in strawberry jam and has certain information?" he asked bluntly.

"S'right" said the boy still grinning.

"Well, what is it?" snapped Baxter.

"Tell you inside." With this the boy sauntered into the cafe followed by a reluctant Baxter whose sheer desperation for winners impelled him to share such obnoxious company.

He sat down opposite the boy, who ordered three cream cakes and a bottle of lemonade from the waitress.

"Right, I'm listening" said Baxter, realising he was about to inherit the bill for these confectionery delights.

"I'm a stable lad in 'Dodgy' Drake's stable" said the boy through a mouthful of cream cake. Baxter regarded the boy with slightly less distaste. 'Dodgy' Drake's stable was sending out a stream of winners and had landed several big gambles. "That's it, I've finished" said the boy looking up from the plate.

"Finished?" queried Baxter. "You haven't said anything yet!"

"Finished me cakes, I 'ave" replied the boy, licking his fingers. Baxter begrudgingly ordered more cakes and told the boy to either eat more slowly or talk faster.

"If you make it worth me while, I can tell you when our 'orses are going to win."

Baxter warmed to the boy, pushed the cakes nearer him and even poured some more lemonade into his glass.

"That's it, I'm finished" said the boy

"We've got one at Kempton this afternoon" said the adolescent piranha as his jaws snapped onto another cake. "See, the guvnor, don't tell us nuffin' and even our jockey don't know what's going on 'til he's in the paddock. So if the horse is going to win, 'e'll touch his boots to tell his mates to get the money on."

Baxter understood perfectly for he had heard about this sort of signaling. Having got the information he wanted, and alarmed by the boy's prodigious appetite, he was anxious to leave. He arranged to see the boy at the racecourse that afternoon and promised him a tenner if the horse won.

There was a bright smile on Baxter's face as he returned to his office for he had just withdrawn the last fifty pounds from his bank account and money in his pocket always had an agreeable effect on him. He was even whistling as he checked the times of the trains to Kempton Park and dusted his binoculars. Why, this new source of information could prove a gold mine, imagined Baxter. His only regret was that he wouldn't know if the horse was going to win until it left the paddock, which was too late to inform his clients.

He arrived at the course like a man sure of his destiny and watched the first two races with the admirable detachment of the disciplined punter. Both the favourites had won easily but nothing could diminish the exhilarating sense of superiority that intoxicates a man with inside information.

'Dodgy' Drake's horse was due to run in the third, so Baxter drifted over to the paddock. He had studied the race carefully and according to Baxter's appraisal of form, the quaintly named The Perfumed Frog was not without a chance. One by one, the horses entered the paddock. The Perfumed Frog was led in by the pimply lad whose complexion, Baxter concluded, was the result of scoffing a multitude of sickly cakes.

The boy acknowledged him with a wink and Baxter decided to see how the bookies rated The Perfumed Frog's chances. The odds were 6 to 1 and Baxter returned to the paddock as the jockeys entered. The jockey for the Drake stable was certainly no stylist and any resemblance between him and Lester Piggott was purely imaginary.

With his eyes almost watering under the strain, Baxter watched his every move. The jockey stood talking earnestly to the owner and trainer and, in Baxter's opinion, seemed to be fidgeting about a lot. Baxter put it down to the tension of being responsible for landing great betting coups.

At last, the bell came for the jockeys to mount and immediately he was seated in The Perfumed Frog's saddle, the jockey touched his boot. Alarm bells rang in Baxter's head. This was it - the signal.

He rushed down to the ring and got forty pounds at 6 to 1. Dashing back to the paddock, he was just in time to see the jockey touch his boots again, but lower down this time. Working on the theory that the lower the touch on the boots the bigger the certainty, Baxter made another bee-line for the bookies. This time he could only get 5 to 1 for his remaining tenner.

The horses were now out on the course and

Baxter, who had his binoculars trained on The Perfumed Frog, again saw the jockey touch his boot.

Baxter was hopping up and down with frustration. The bookies were all lined up to be slaughtered and he had run out of ammunition.

He took another look at the boards. Somebody must have been piling the money on because The Perfumed Frog's odds were now 3 to 1. The horses were at the start when the jockey put his hand down and touched his boot around the ankle. "Lend me some money!" Baxter wanted to scream out. Here he had the biggest certainty since King Canute got his feet wet and all he had on it was fifty pounds.

Whilst seriously considering the possibility of depositing his gold watch with a bookie as security for another bit on The Perfumed Frog, the announcement came that they were off.

The Perfumed Frog was always up with the leaders and as they came round into the straight he was lying third and coasting. Baxter's brain began to embark on the delightful mathematical exercise of working out his winnings.

Any time now, he expected his money to hit the front and quickstep past the winning post. However, The Perfumed Frog did not seem to be making much headway on the two in front and Baxter began thinking that the jockey was leaving it a bit late. He was still thinking that when they passed the post with The Perfumed Frog still lying third.

Baxter performed an amusing war dance on his betting tickets and stormed over to the unsaddling enclosure, where the boy was putting a cloth over the sweating horse.

"'Ello" he said, wondering why on earth Baxter was pulling such horrible faces. "Bit of a waste of time, wasn't it? They never fancied The Perfumed Frog today."

"Never fancied it!" ranted Baxter. "Don't give me that baloney! I saw all the signals. The jockey touched his boots four of five times at least!"

"Oh that wasn't a signal" explained the boy calmly "it's just that 'e's got new boots."

"New boots!" exploded Baxter. "New boots!"

This racing story is not about Baxter but about a character named Hymie whom he knew well. Whenever Baxter is down on his luck - which is often - he will sometimes recall this story to remind him that things could always be a lot worse.

HYMIE IS A LOSER, MY LIFE

Hymie was standing on the racecourse, gripping his betting ticket and waiting with intense anxiety for the announcement of the photo finish. At last, a rather regal voice said, "First..." - Hymie held his breath - "number five."

It clearly wasn't Hymie's horse because he gave a strangulated whine through clenched teeth, tore the ticket up into confetti-like pieces, threw them down and proceeded to stomp over them in a style seen only in the coolest discos. Hymie though, was unsuitably in his late fifties and the exertions left him looking distraught. He shuffled over to a kindly-looking, grey-haired bookmaker of the same age.

"Abe, soon I will have to surrender" said Hymie sadly. "I like you, you are a fair bookmaker but to me you are unlucky. Never in all my days of racing, do I ever back so many losers as since I am betting with you."

Hymie was so exasperated he was having to collect his thoughts.

"If I back the favourite, it gets beat. If I oppose the favourite, it wins. There is a photo finish - mine is second. Even when I do back a winner, there is an objection and it gets disqualified. Ple-a-s-e" Hymie said hysterically "what must I do to back a winner with you?"

"I don't know" said Abe sympathetically. "You see, Hymie, some punters are just mugs and some are unlucky. Right now, you couldn't win a kick in a riot."

"But is this right?" appealed Hymie. "For a man who every day spends three tortuous hours studying the form book and the slippery ways of trainers and jockeys, do I not deserve better?"

Abe stuffed a large cigar into his mouth and forgot to offer one to Hymie.

"You do" he said "but what do I say? Do I tell you that you should bet with someone else because I am unlucky to you? You are good business to me, Hymie, and always you pay. Last week, you know, you lose £300 so I order a new colour T.V. Now, whenever I watch it, I think of you. It is nice that way."

Hymie didn't think it was nice that way at all but he did have an admission to make.

"I can't stop betting with you, Abe - you see it's an obsession. It's more than just wanting my money back, I've got to prove I can beat you."

"Ah, well" said Abe, pulling his board down and preparing to go "it's up to you, but be grateful for something - at least, you have your health."

"My health, I have. My money, you have" replied Hymie, refusing to be consoled.

Abe took the cigar from his mouth and placed his hand affectionately on Hymie's shoulder.

"I don't like to see you looking so unhappy Hymie, so I hope you back a winner." He moved off but called back "Just a little one!"

Hymie was still disconsolate as he walked his way to the station. Around him there were other race-goers chattering about their misfortunes or good luck. He looked to the road when Abe gave him a friendly toot from the seat of his Rolls Royce. Abe lived about half a mile from Hymie but Hymie tried hard not to think about it.

At home that evening, Hymie told his wife that he was unwell and went to bed early. After much experience, she correctly interpreted this to mean he'd done his money and was fed up.

However, even in the sub-conscious, Hymie's mind must have turned to horseracing for at two o'clock in the morning he awoke very excited, having just seen a horse named Gezuntheit win the Ascot Gold Cup by six lengths. Having been told by his wife to stop fidgeting and get back in bed, Hymie lay there stoically suppressing his excitement.

Finally, at what he judged was the earliest reasonable hour, he got up and went to his racing books. The Gold Cup was two weeks away and, to Hymie's amazement, a horse named Gezuntheit was entered to run. The reason the horse was unknown to him was not just because it was trained in France but the animal had not run for over a year.

However, Hymie's optimism remained undiminished. When did he ever dream a winner? Uncle Morpheus had come to his salvation.

When Abe Freeman entered his office that morning, his phone was bawling like an unattended baby.

"It's me, Hymie" said a voice in an unusually

"At 2 a.m. he awoke very excited"

high key "what price you lay me Gezuntheit in the Gold Cup?"

Abe consulted his list.

"Fifties" he said.

"A hundred to win " shouted Hymie.

"You know something?" asked Abe.

"Do I ever know anything?" retorted Hymie squeakily. "I have a cold and keep sneezing, that's all."

"See you at the races later?" enquired Abe. "I'm at Epsom."

"No" said Hymie. "No more racing until after the Gold Cup."

Hymie kept his word. Somehow, he felt he was right about Gezuntheit. He was becoming a much more agreeable person now that horseracing and betting wasn't souring his day. His wife loved the change in Hymie and the dog was actually taken for a walk. Having lived such a sedentary life however, the initial excursion proved too much for the overweight canine and after carrying it back from the park, an exhausted Hymie resolved to put the animal on a diet.

But nothing could dilute Hymie's new-found harmony because an incredible thing had happened - he had managed to dream the race again! The result had not only been the same but the pitfalls of objections and disqualification were no longer worries because this time he'd seen a Gallic gentleman receive the prize.

During the following weeks, Hymie placed two more bets with Abe, which would win him £15000 and which he reckoned was just about the amount he'd lost to Abe over the years.

Come the day of the Gold Cup, and

Gezuntheit's price was down to 10 to 1. Hymie was at the course feeling unusually confident. He stood near Abe's pitch with a constant smile on his face, which Abe found slightly unsettling. Abe most definitely didn't appear his usual cheerful self, particularly when the big race started.

Well, some dreams do come true and Hymie's certainly did. Gezuntheit trotted up by six lengths.

"Got you at last, Abe!" shouted Hymie. "You're not a *boch* after all."

"It's a lot of money you have won" said Abe seriously.

"I hope you hedge" offered Hymie.

Abe shook his head.

"I wish now I hedge but always you lose."

"Until now! Until now!" repeated Hymie. "And so when do I get my cheque?"

"You will have it first post on Monday" was the muted reply.

Hymie understood and Abe was an honest man. Hymie lit a fat cigar, forgot to offer one to Abe, and walked off like a man who has fulfilled his highest ambition.

At home, Hymie's wife was in the kitchen wearing an unattractive apron and the only sound from the radio was a reading of the news. She was, therefore, unprepared for Hymie's sudden desire to drag her into the dining room and waltz her around the floor to the accompaniment of his humming.

She probably thought he'd been drinking and, if she did, she said the right thing to sober him up.

"By the way, I tidied up your writing desk

today and cleared out all those bits of paper you left lying around."

Hymie went white, abandoned his wife in the middle of a spin turn and fled to his study. Except for the blotting pad, the desk was clear. There was no sign of his voucher receipts for his bets on Gezunheit.

He came back to his wife, his words almost hoarse. "Where......?"

She pointed outside to the dustbin. It was empty - the dustmen had been. Hymie returned frantic, made a fair imitation of strangling his wife and vented his feelings by screwing the neck of an ancient fox fur lying conveniently on the sideboard.

Throughout the following weekend, Hymie tried hard to overcome his profound unease. Abe was an honest man and, anyway, how could he deny that he'd laid Hymie the bets when he had already promised that his cheque would arrive first thing on Monday. It would be alright, he told himself, but then Abe had always somehow been...well,.....the thought felt like an ice-cream on the back of his neck.....well, Abe had always somehow been unlucky to him.

On Monday morning, Hymie was studying the letterbox of his door like a retriever waiting for a grouse to fall. One letter arrived but, alas, it wasn't Abe's cheque but a bill.

Hymie rang Abe Freeman's number. The muffled voice of his secretary answered it.

"I'm afraid Mr Freeman passed away on Saturday evening" she said tearfully. "If you wish to send flowers........."

THE COMPUTER CHALLENGE

Baxter was in the purple valleys of despair. The cause was simple and familiar. A 2-year-old colt given out to his clients had run like a goat. Its winning chance, which had been heralded on his tipping line with full orchestral accompaniment, should, on reflection, have been played in a minor key as a piccolo solo.

Baxter's hope that its next entry would be to a veterinary hospital for a gelding operation was more practical than unkind for it meant that its impoverished seed would not be passed on to create more slow-running creatures on which he and his clients could do their brains.

His usual equanimity was still absent when he arrived at his office the next morning. The desultory collection of post that awaited him - two bookmaker's accounts demanding money, an offer from a finance company of loans at a rate that would have made Shylock blush and finally a pizza flyer – were all viewed with equal disregard. Baxter didn't even like pizzas and considered them a very expensive variant of cheese on toast.

He made his coffee and opened up his racing paper with as much relish as a person with toothache would regard a Granny Smith. He glanced at the sheets in a subdued manner until a full-page advertisement nearly knocked his eyes out. It screamed

WIN BUNDLES! WINNER AFTER WINNER with COMPUTER ANALYSIS of SELECTED RACES

Every influence in a race is analysed – weight, time-rating, going, track, jockey, current form and fitness. **DON'T WASTE TIME** with Systems, Staking Plans and old-fashioned tipping services (SureFire,etc.)

TOP TECH is UNIQUE, **TOP TECH** is the BEST, **TOP TECH** is the ULTIMATE TOOL in the quest for WINNERS. DON'T MISS this opportunity of a TAX-FREE INCOME for LIFE. **STOP LOSING - START WINNING.**

The copy was clearly composed with a blow-torch and ended with a telephone number whose numerals were of a size normally reserved for railway platforms.

But it was the personal attack that startled Baxter. He didn't regard his business as old-fashioned even if the brown cardigan and bedroom slippers its proprietor relaxed in at home were not quite the attire of the modern man. He rang the paper's advertising department to complain. They apologised - it had slipped through their censorship.

Baxter remained unhappy - the damage had been done and the perpetrator was clearly a charlatan. Computer analysis to find winners, sniffed Baxter - what a load of drivel. As race-winning was never an exact science it was clearly codswallop. Unfortunately punters would believe it because their gullibility knew no bounds - if it had, then Baxter himself would have been out of business.

Over the next few days, Baxter suffered the slow agony of a man who has inadvertently hung himself on a bungee rope. The scorching copy advertising Top Tech's successes was now filling several pages. The claims were hysterical. Soon clients 'would be millionaires', bookmakers 'would be cycling to the course' and the most recent stated that 'Beachey Head had erected signs reading 'NO MORE BOOKMAKERS ALLOWED'.

It was all nonsense of course but it got attention and the undeniable fact was that Top Tech was finding a winner every day. They were invariably favourites and short prices but they did win. It was June, the ground was firm, small fields predominated but Baxter himself couldn't give a winner. There were no new subscribers and his premium rate line was so quiet, he kept checking to see if it was still connected.

In desperation, Baxter phoned Top Tech for himself. A cultured voice gave him two options.

"Press 1 if you are a first-time caller, press 2 if you are already a winner and want to win some more".

Baxter's wish for a third option - to smack the proprietor in the mouth - was unavailable.

He pressed 1, whereupon the attractive speaker introduced himself. There followed a list of his academic achievements at Harrow, Oxford and Harvard culminating in a degree in Computer Engineering.

Baxter had his watch on the desk calculating how much this useless information was costing him. After four minutes, the subject of racing was reached with an 'on the spot' report from Kempton Park.

This included a detailed weather report, state of the going, a description of the local scenery and a mass of trivia whose only omission was the holiday arrangements for the Clerk of the Course. Baxter's impatience was at its crescendo when at last the horse was announced. Baxter slammed down the phone.

"Seven minutes!" he yelled. Seven minutes to give a 5 to 4 chance that 95% of racing hacks will have tipped! How does he get away with it?"

Mrs Wilbow entered. "You alright Mr Baxter? Sounds like you're having a turn."

"No, I'm not having a turn" said Baxter who discerned that the visit was more to do with overdue rent than a genuine inquiry about his health.

There was an uncomfortable silence as both parties eyed each other. Finally the woman folded her arms. "I don't like to mention......"

"Mrs Wilbow" interrupted Baxter "you may not be aware but a rival to my racing service has emerged. He's rather successful at the moment and my business is suffering - someone calling himself Will Bow. Good Heavens, that's your name too!" It was the first time Baxter had realised this.

"That's my nephew, William. He's got an office round the corner in Charlotte Street" said the landlady.

"Yes, I vaguely remember him. Used to visit you years ago. A fair-haired lad always running up and down the stairs making a lot of noise."

"He didn't like you, Mr Baxter. You were always telling him off."

"Well, he was a nuisance" said Baxter with a complete absence of understanding children.

"He came to see me recently and asked me about your business - said it was money for old rope."

"He's a charlatan, Mrs Wilbow - an opportunist, a smart alec."

"I know and he's got degrees to prove it!" She nodded her head like an auctioneer's gavel finalising a sale and left the room.

Baxter tried to get back to his paper but when the humming of his refrigerator started to get on his nerves he gave up. He left a 'no selection today' message for any remaining stoic or masochist among his clients, downed a glass of malt and set off for the premises of Top Tech.

It was a suite in a small but smart office block. Baxter looked through the glass. There was a central computer, several monitors and a seemingly over-worked answering machine assembly. There was also a typist in one corner who, seeing Baxter, went into a side office.

A door besides Baxter opened. "Why Mr Baxter, I wondered if curiosity would get the better of you."

Baxter recognised the fair-haired, wide-eared infant nuisance even if this was an enlarged version.

"So you're William Wilbow or Will Bow - quite clever that."

"Baxter looked through the glass"

"It's all clever stuff, Mr Baxter. Come into my office. As you can see the main office is rather busy and quite noisy." The young man guided Baxter into a small room and shut the door. "So how's business, Mr Baxter?"

"Good" lied Baxter.

"My aunt tells me your behind with the rent."

"Did she now" replied Baxter. "It's sad when their marbles start to go."

"I must be hurting you, Mr Baxter. I've given eight consecutive winners - there's no way you can match that."

"You're not a racing man" said Baxter. "You're an impostor who knows nothing about the game."

"I don't need to. I feed in all the form, the weights, the stats, everything - even the local weather report - and out comes the winner."

"Yes, the favourite! 2 to 1 would be an outsider to you!"

"But they win Mr Baxter - that's what's important" concluded the young man, who despite his veneer of courtesy towards Baxter also managed to convey an impression of dislike.

"You're just on a roll" argued Baxter. "You need insight, you need to know racing and the people in it."

"You know something, Mr Baxter. I have never been to a racecourse in my life. Never sat on a horse, never bet on a horse. I've no interest in horseracing as a sport, only as a business."

"So today's taped report from Kempton Park was baloney?"

"Let's say imaginative" said his rival.

Baxter shook his head sadly and left without another word.

He felt better for his visit and was reassured that he was dealing with an arrogant upstart and not a genius. The trouble was that business was bad and his tipping line was about as popular as lockjaw at a gossip columnists' convention. A little later, the level of his whisky bottle had dipped by two fluid ounces when he learned that the Top Tech selection had won yet again.

Baxter's luck finally changed when Poultry in Motion, a soured 8-year-old handicapper who hadn't won for two years but who had just changed stables, was tipped to him by his Lambourn contact. At 50 to 1, even Baxter was surprised and having even backed the equine Lazarus himself, he could afford to tell racing that Baxter was back doing the business.

In went a full-page ad, specifically adjacent to the one for Top Tech. Fighting fire with fire, Baxter's prose was personal but proud.

SUREFIRE, THE KING OF TIPPING, STILL REIGNS!
IMPOSTERS to his crown(Top Tech, etc.) will be **VANQUISHED.**
SUREFIRE sends out 50-1 shells to pound the bookies not 5/4 pellets!

Baxter's clients returned as the run continued with 10 to 1, 8 to 1 and a couple of 9 to 2 chances all winning. Top Tech also kept its own run going including a 5 to 2 chance, which it indecently described, as 'massive'.

The ads were getting more personal all the time. Set side by side the pages were becoming must-read attractions in themselves. It was turning into a soap opera with readers wanting to know who was coming out on top. Other sectors of the media became interested and started to cover the hostilities. People were taking sides and the pressure to keep finding winners was enormous on Baxter. Information from people who appeared to want to help had to be considered carefully in case they were Top Tech supporters trying to slip him a 'wrong 'un'.

Business was frantic with punters ringing up both tipping lines. Newspapers welcomed the increased sales with their advertising departments fuelling the rivalry by suggesting even more exaggerated and belligerent copy. It was all good stuff but it couldn't last and there had to be a showdown.

It came in an unexpected way. Just days before the Ascot July meeting, Top Tech announced that it's bet of the season was in the Princess Margaret Stakes. Futhermore, it challenged SureFire to oppose its selection and promised to close down its business if the horse lost provided SureFire agreed to the same if its own selection was beaten.

It was confrontational stuff but much as Baxter was tempted by the opportunity to outfox his adversary, he wasn't foolhardy. Looking at the entries for the race it was quite clear that Brick Tent would be the Top Tech tip. It was far and away the best 2 year old filly to appear that season and would start big odds-on in a field of six. The only possible danger seemed East Smithfield who'd been beaten a comfortable 3 lengths by Brick Tent in its first run.

So although Baxter didn't conclude that Brick Tent was an absolute certainty, he wasn't up to sacrificing his business to oppose it. He therefore maintained a silence on the challenge but gave a sneaky call to his rival.

Brick Tent was indeed the tip provided the ground remained good to fast and Top Tech was refraining from giving any further selections until after the Princess Margaret Stakes. 'Save it up for a royal touch' was its excruciating poetic advice.

It was the end of the first day's racing at Ascot's July Meeting. Thankfully he'd given his clients the winner of the Rated Stakes race but apart from that Baxter had done no good. As he was leaving, a horsebox had arrived at the stabling area and disembarking from it was Brick Tent covered by her trainer's initialled blanket.

Just to confirm this, he asked the lad leading the horse. The unsmiling lad simply nodded.

Baxter was elated - he'd planned for such an eventuality. He rang the advertising departments of the racing press.

"Run advertisement B - I'm opposing Top Tech - challenge accepted!"

They were delighted - crunch time had arrived!

The publicity was superb. The 'Racing Post' even had a mention on its front page 'SureFire Takes up Challenge'. Inside was Baxter's advertisement.

BRICK TENT CANNOT WIN -
GOODBYE TOP TECH
PRINCESS MARGARET STAKES
WINNER GIVEN IN 60 SECONDS
RING SUREFIRE - THE GREATEST
TIPPING SERVICE EVER!

It was compelling stuff and although Baxter was confident, he couldn't be sure.

But come the day and the race went like a dream. Baxter had told all his clients to go for East Smithfield and she won 1/2 length from an unraced Middleham filly with Brick Tent a disappointing last. For Top Tech it wasn't just defeat but ignominy.

Receiving congratulations and doing press interviews were surprisingly exhausting, concluded Baxter as he left the train at Waterloo.

A little later the beckoning sign of the Drover's Arms offered the refreshment he felt he deserved. He ordered a Macallan, his favourite malt, and looked around the bar. In the corner was the slumped figure of Mrs Wilbow's nephew whose face had the pessimistic look of a Brighton hotelier consulting the long-range weather forecast.

"Don't worry, lad, there's other things you can do. I wish I had your prospects" said Baxter.

The young man looked up. "But where did I go wrong, Baxter? I fed every piece of relevant information into that machine and Brick Tent came out lengths clear every time. To finish last was unbelievable."

"Not really" said Baxter. "You see the one

piece of information it didn't have was the sort you only get by being on the spot and I happened to be at Ascot when Brick Tent arrived for stabling."

"And what happened?"

"Well," said Baxter "I heard it cough."

TRADING IN WINNERS

It was to Baxter's regret that trainers rarely rang him up with information. The top trainers didn't need Baxter and were probably even unaware of his existence. The few that did were small gambling trainers wanting a commission executed or expecting something in return. They were reliably unreliable and had a strong tendency to overrate the ability of their horses. Parsons was such a trainer.

"Parsons here" said the voice.

"Oh, yes" said Baxter nonchalantly.

Had it been Aidan O'Brien, he'd have whipped out a prayer mat and taken the call with justified reverence.

"Are you going to Epsom today?"

"Of course" replied Baxter – the Surrey racecourse was one of his favourites.

"That's good because I've got one lined up for the 6 furlong sprint there - Gorilla Lipstick. Have £500 on it."

"You said that last time" reminded Baxter. "Last race at Warwick and the only thing it beat was the sunset – and that was close."

"Yes, but this time, *I'm* having £500 on it" emphasised the trainer.

Baxter listened in silence.

"We've never had the horse right before

because he had this muscle spasm in his back that we didn't know about. Well, that's now been sorted and he's a different horse. He'll be a big price tomorrow."

"Yours usually are" said Baxter unkindly.

"Look, Baxter, I haven't got the readies myself so d'you think you could put the bet on for me? You'll get a nice drink out of it and should the worse happen you know you'll get the money."

This was true. Parsons had always paid Baxter but it was invariably over a long period in which time Parsons presumably hoped amnesia would set in to the lender.

While not exactly fired up with enthusiasm, Baxter had to acknowledge that Parsons did occasionally come up with the goods. As a trainer who averaged about 10 winners a year, it was the only way the man could survive.

Fortunately, Baxter was holding a few quid from a recent winning spell and was a fervent follower of the maxim 'speculate to accumulate' despite a recurring misgiving that the originator of this principle had probably died skint.

It was early morning and Baxter had still to immerse himself in a study of the form for Epsom. It looked a difficult card and none more so than the sprint handicap for which Gorilla Lipstick was entered. The horse was not without a chance on some earlier form but it wasn't too well drawn and would need some luck in running. On the positive side, it was going to be a big price.

Baxter finished his study and was about to make himself a coffee when Mrs Wilbow suddenly burst into song as she began her morning cleaning. His landlady's voice was about as melodious as a whistling kettle and Baxter decided instead to pour himself a drop of Macallan for fortitude.

The question was what to put up on his tipping line. He strongly fancied one in the opening race but it was well exposed and was going to be favourite – on the other hand, a winner was a winner. The only other information he'd had was Gorilla Lipstick, which was decidedly dubious. It wasn't really such a difficult choice. Most punters thought they could pick out short-priced winners – it was the big prices that impressed them, so Gorilla Lipstick it was.

The train lurched slowly into the station at Epsom. It was a glorious August day, as Baxter joined the bustling crowd heading for the racecourse. Like himself, they were all invigorated by the promise of an afternoon's racing even though the majority were, in fact, embarking on a charitable mission to swell the coffers of the bookmakers who viewed their arrival with the sort of smile with which the Borgias had greeted their dinner guests.

It was just inside the entrance that Baxter saw the curious sight of a person bedecked in umbrellas. Behind the array of various covers – some open, some closed – a deep but anonymous voice was calling out.

"Get your umbrellas, 'ere! Fifty bob each, only fifty bob!"

The deep voice sounded familiar to Baxter.

"Is that you behind there, Joey?"

A face emerged, wearing an impenetrable pair of sunglasses and frown lines that resembled a taxi driver stuck in traffic with an empty cab.

"Course it's me, who d'you think it is, Margot Fonteyn?"

"What on earth are you doing selling umbrellas on a day like this?"

"Can't 'elp it if it's sunny, can I? Umbrellas, fifty bob each!"

Joey's enterprise as a seller of umbrellas puzzled Baxter as it was not his line at all. Joey was a disappearing breed - the racecourse tout. He was invariably hard up and a bit of a character into the bargain – not altogether unlike Baxter but more downmarket.

However, Baxter knew for a fact that luck had been kind to Joey lately for only a few days before he'd told Baxter he was going to back a horse which had won at 33-1.

"Come on Joey, don't tell me you've got no money."

"You think I'd be doing this otherwise? Umbrellas, fifty bob each!"

"But I thought you backed the 33-I chance that trotted up at Windsor?"

"Don't talk to me about that" replied the umbrella stand with disgust. "You ask that Dave Donovan, the bookie."

It was clear that Joey was not in the best of moods.

"What d'you fancy today, Joey?" asked Baxter changing the subject.

"Rain" said Joey flatly. "Umbrellas, fifty bob each!"

"Umbrellas, fifty bob each!"

Baxter turned to walk away but hesitated.

"By the way, Joey we've gone decimalised now - two pounds fifty might make more sense."

"Umbrellas, fifty bob each!" shouted Joey defiantly.

Baxter backed the favourite he fancied in the first race and the animal looked all over the winner until it was passed by a colt who flew the final 200 yards like it was being pursued by a vet with a gelding tool.

The only consolation, as he tore up his ticket, was that he hadn't served it up to his clients.

The next race wasn't any better when an old nag that hadn't won for two years put its best foot forward and got up in a photo. Baxter's could only surmise that the only explanation for its improved running was that the trainer had pinned up a photo of the local knacker's yard in its box.

A line of bookies displaying beaming smiles was an odious sight to Baxter and prominent amongst them was Dave Donovan. Baxter rather envied the man for he had inherited a chain of department stores as a young man and, still only thirty, was a multi-millionaire who had taken to bookmaking as a form of amusement. It was all right for some, thought Baxter.

Gorilla Lipstick was 14's in places but generally 16-1. It seemed a fair price to Baxter and ferrying about the ring he didn't have any problem in getting the £500 on in small parcels. Then quite quickly, the price began to shrivel up as something of a gamble began to take place. Baxter was occasionally led by instinct and this was such a moment. Gorilla

Lipstick was going to win – it was such an overwhelming conclusion to Baxter that he took all the remaining cash from his wallet and plunged in to take 8's from the one remaining bookmaker showing it.

The horse had looked great in the paddock and Parsons had clearly laid the horse out for the race. At the off, it was 7-1 clear favourite but with the jockey slowly tacking across to get a position and the horse going very easily it looked like the biggest give-away since a bookmaker – later committed – offered dual forecasts for the Boat Race.

And then it happened, the rider lost an iron when a leather snapped, the horse became unbalanced, lost its momentum and was beaten a neck.

Baxter was suffering that feeling that only the truly vanquished punter could understand. He wondered indeed if Lady Luck was a lady at all. If so, a slap in the face would probably been the extent of her displeasure. Instead, Baxter felt as if he'd been kneed in the groin, had his arm twisted behind his back, been run into a wall and finished off with a good kicking. A sadistic Amazon was far more likely, decided Baxter. The feeling was that of having had all the stuffing knocked out of him.

All he wanted to do was go home. As he made his way to the gate, he saw Joey again. He was sitting down, studying a paper but still surrounded by umbrellas. He looked up as Baxter approached.

"Going already? There's a good thing in this next race – Umpire's Finger."

"No money, Joey. Done my lot in that last race. Absolutely cleaned out."

"You don't need money to bet with Donovan. 'Ow much your binoculars worth?"

"Twenty quid maybe" he said without much thought.

"They'll do then. Give me them and you've got a bet – this 'orse will win!"

Before Baxter knew what was happening, Joey had removed the bins from around his neck and was heading towards the ring. He felt so dismal he didn't understand or much care what Joey was up to.

Although he could not see the race from where he was, he heard the course commentator call home Umpire's Finger as the winner and the price was12 to 1.

Fifteen minutes later, Joey returned.

"E's done it to me again!" he said with disgust.

"Done what?" asked Baxter

"Well, when I backed that 33-1 winner the other day, I didn't have no money. What I did have though was an umbrella and Donovan said 'e'd take that instead."

Baxter was beginning to understand.

"Don't tell me he paid you out in umbrellas?"

"'E jolly well did," said Joey "'ere's your binoculars back and 'ere's the 12 pairs you won off him. I'm going to Newbury tomorrow, you can stand next to me if you want."

CORPORATE TIPPING

Baxter was at his desk in the milieu of junk and rubbish that constituted the office of the SureFire Tipping Service. To one side of him was the Nottingham card of the 'Racing Post' while on the other side he was absorbing the details of Smiling Egyptian that appeared in his well-ploughed copy of 'Horses in Training'.

There were times during his study of form that Baxter was so absorbed that any greeting from Mrs Wilbow simply passed his antennae. His landlady sensed that this was such an occasion.

She had swept the staircase and was now holding a duster and a spray of furniture polish as she watched him through the open door of the office. Feeling playful, she took a pen from her pinafore pocket and wrote on a piece of paper 'Morning, Mr Baxter'. She took a hazardous route avoiding various obstacles of litter and placed it on his desk. Baxter picked it up, turned it over and wrote 'Morning Mrs Wilbow'. His landlady smiled, put the piece of paper back in her pinafore pocket and turned away.

Because of the proliferation of debris it was almost impossible to clean the office and Mrs Wilbow simply sprayed and dusted around the door to mark a trace of her presence. It was this token gesture that caused Baxter's nose to twitch with the rapidity of a rabbit.

"That's a very pleasant smell" said Baxter looking up.

"My new polish," explained Mrs Wilbow "beautiful isn't it?"

"Uhm-m" agreed Baxter, his nose still twitching with the fragrance.

"Everyone likes it" went on the landlady. "It's advertised on the tele a lot – it costs a bit more than my old polish but it's a lovely smell."

Baxter was equally intoxicated with the chances of Smiling Egyptian in the 4 o'clock race at Nottingham and decided to put it up on his tipping line. It was a reasonable card at the Midlands track and Baxter was keen to go and back the horse on course.

He had just ensconced himself into his train seat at St.Pancras when a large man with several double chins and blood pressure showing in his cheeks, opened the carriage door and threw himself down opposite Baxter. The long, loud sound of a guard's whistle followed immediately.

"You just made it, Jake" smiled Baxter.

The man held out his hand.

"Well, well, Baxter, my old mate! How are you?"

Jake Morris had run a tipping service himself some year's back but had suffered the ignominy of the longest losing run that Baxter had ever heard of. This feat had been achieved despite including a majority of favourites, several odds-on chances from 4-5 to 4-11 and even the loser of a two-horse race. His half-century of losers had only been avoided when a 4's on chance had got up in a photo finish. Of course, at this point his clients no longer cared as they had all either shot themselves or taken up careers as beggars.

His career as a racehorse tipster seemed over and his name was something of a byword for incompetence. It was therefore with some amazement that Baxter learnt how Jake was still in the tipping game.

"Well" explained Jake "I now call myself 'The Captain' and I'm a corporate tipster."

"I've heard of that" said Baxter. "How's it work?"

"It's sweet, it really is. First you need an amusing patter that will entertain people. Then you get on the books of an agency that organises these corporate days out and offer your services as a tipster. It's great. You give 'em your selections for the afternoon and even if they get beat you don't get slaughtered as in your business. As long as you've been entertaining and can give 'em at least one winner, they're happy."

"Uhm-m" said Baxter doubtfully. He didn't see himself as an entertainer unless you counted his antics when he backed a 157 or got beat in a photo.

"And the money's great - £300 for an afternoon's work" added Jake. "Fancy a drink?"

When they got to the racecourse, Jake said "By the way, what's your tip for today?"

"Smiling Egyptian in the two miler" said Baxter.

"Got to have things his own way and too much weight, anyway – can't fancy it myself" offered

Jake and hurried off.

Baxter wasn't too dismayed. Jake probably never fancied Ribot in any of its races either.

However, a little after 4 o'clock, Baxter had the uneasy but familiar feeling that always overtook him when his horse was not going well. Smiling Egyptian had been pushed along the whole way round and seemed as tractable as a punctured wheelbarrow. There were still two furlongs to go when Baxter screwed his betting ticket up in disgust. He'd made an expensive misjudgement and it hadn't been a good day.

It was in the buffet bar on the way back to London that Jake joined him.

"Ah Baxter, glad I've seen you. Pretty good day today – two out of three I tipped 'em. Both short but who cares about that!"

"Good luck to you" said Baxter generously.

"I want you to help me out actually. Can you believe it, I've got two of these corporate functions on the same date next week, Chester and Goodwood. I can't do both so if I take Chester, you could do Goodwood for me. I'll give you £250 up front. It'll be a doddle for a racing man like you." He looked closely at Baxter. "You might have to smile a bit more, though."

Jake had a persuasive way with people and besides Baxter needed the money so it was always odds-on he'd be at Goodwood the following Wednesday. In fact, he'd quite warmed to the idea. He was still going racing and still doing his normal job of tipping horses but this time to a live audience.

The day was warm and pleasant and a Baxter

of slightly improved appearance went to his office as normal. He was quite looking forward to his daily 'fix' of Polygleam which Mrs Wilbow informed him was the name of the spray which continued to titillate his nose.

Baxter had studied the Goodwood card the previous night and decided it was too hard. He had received no information either and while a 'no selection today' message was all right for his tipping line, it was essential he come up with some recommendations for the corporate clients.

He was no nearer solving this problem when he arrived at the corporate box and introduced himself to Mr Queensbury, the chairman of Tempest Holdings. He was a small energetic man of Baxter's age, with a wild mass of hair like a shoal of lion-fish around his head. He puffed a large cigar and impressed Baxter at once by asking him what his favourite drink was and finding that no Macallan was available, immediately dispatched his chauffeur to fetch a bottle from somewhere.

Meanwhile, Baxter addressed a crowd of twenty – mainly men – and told them a little about himself before going through the runners in the huge field for the first race. He seemed to have their attention and was going rather well until a little woman in a big hat piped up impatiently.

"So which one do we back, Mr Baxter?"

It was then that he realised he didn't have a clue - there were so many with chances. He couldn't tell them it was too hard and to keep their money in their pockets for these people were here to enjoy themselves and have some action. Baxter hesitated.

"Well," he looked at the bottle of Macallan which had suddenly appeared on the table beside him and saw the price label of £19.75 "I think we should go for number 19".

"But you never mentioned that one" a voice complained.

"It's like a beauty contest – the winner is announced last" responded Baxter, who hadn't seriously considered Eskimo Garden despite the openness of the race.

Soon there were calls of £50 and even £100 on Eskimo Garden. Baxter blanched. These people were steaming in as if he were some sort of prophet. He poured a drop of malt into his glass and just hoped for a decent run from the animal so that he didn't look a complete idiot.

However, it appeared that Baxter was indeed a prophet for Eskimo Garden won in a tight finish at 12-1. There was much hooting and hollering as the crowd re-grouped. Smiling faces surrounded him and patted him on the back. He couldn't tell them it was a fluke - he'd become the Prince of Tipsters.

The second race was a smaller field of nine handicappers but just as trappy as the first race. Baxter's confidence was high and those present were hanging onto his every word. He commented on each runner but already knew what his selection was going to be. Why desert the winning formula contained in the £19.75 price label of the Macallan bottle? The next selection had to be number 7, a horse named Whistling Duck. Again it had a reasonable chance although

Baxter would never have tipped it normally as the jockey was one who Baxter considered could give a bike a bad back.

Slow start, bad jockey, a price drift out to 7-1 but Whistling Duck still managed to win. Grins as wide as the Grand Canyon greeted Baxter after the race and he could feel the warmth of admiring gazes. Mr Queensbury stuffed a large cigar into Baxter's breast pocket and said it was the best afternoon's racing he'd ever had. Baxter felt he'd ascended the throne of tipsterdom. He was King.

By the time of the third race, Baxter had imbibed so much Macallan, his analysis of the race was not quite so clear in his mind. It mattered very little, though, because his audience was totally behind him and, following the seemingly invincible formula, the choice was number 5 on the race card.

Even in his state of increasing intoxication and sky-high confidence, Baxter was able to acknowledge to himself that Rain in the Bedroom was certainly not a horse to lump on. Its form was erratic and the horse had run poorly at Gooodwood before. What it did have going for it was a trainer who had more tricks in him than 'The Conjurors' Handbook'. Whether it was the trainer's money or the bets from Baxter's disciples, Rain in the Bedroom was slammed in to 5-2, having been 4-1 earlier, and sluiced in like an odds-on shot.

The box of Tempest Holdings was a riot of laughter, shouting and celebration. Baxter had achieved an incredible 3 out of 3 with accumulative odds of 363 to 1. King of Tipsters? Emperor, more like it!

"Mr Queensbury stuffed a large cigar into his breast pocket"

Fantastic, genius, unbelievable were just some of the words swirling about in the heady atmosphere. Ten, twenty and even fifty-pound notes were being stuffed into his hand. It was as good as Baxter had ever felt even though he'd not backed a single one of the selections.

"It's been an incredible day, Baxter – I don't know how you do it. Everyone's won money and we're absolutely delighted – It's been really great."

Mr Queensbury stuck another cigar in Baxter's breast pocket because the previous one was being smoked with great enjoyment by the man of the moment.

However, Baxter was finding it extremely difficult to maintain a vertical position any longer and the 10-year malt had befuddled both his speech and thought. He explained in an amusing but drunken style that he was retiring for the rest of the afternoon. Mr Queensbury realising that Baxter was well above the Plimsoll line of intoxication, glanced at the impoverished bottle of Macallan and frowned.

Then suddenly the sky outside the window appeared quite dark. There was a flash of lightning followed by a clap of thunder. Soon a deluge of rain was obscuring the view of the course.

Racing was delayed once, twice and then finally postponed. It was all wonderfully convenient for by now the font of wisdom had dried up but by no means dried out and was slumped in a chair, head back and mouth agape.

By 5.30 p.m. the corporate box was empty apart from Baxter and Mr Queensbury. The chairman of Tempest Holdings got Baxter to wake up and allowed him a few moments to establish his bearings. Baxter had sobered up reasonably well although his head contained a bongo drum which felt like it was being beaten by a native whose house was on fire and who was trying to alert the local fire brigade.

"I want you to know we've all had a wonderful day, Baxter, and I can't thank you enough. What I can do, however, is to urge you to buy our shares. The way we're going at the moment, I can see the share price doubling within six months. Don't forget about it when you get home - take my advice."

He then passed Baxter a large, and expensive-looking business card while Baxter responded by writing his phone number on the back of a till receipt he'd found in his pocket.

Baxter's inspirational run of luck proved to be short-lived because the following week, the SureFire Tipping Service gave four consecutive losers before getting a favourite home. Then another losing run of three before striking again – in fact, it was business as usual. Neither did he hear anymore from a dumbfounded Jake who apparently considered Baxter had set an impossible target for every other corporate tipster. And, of course, he disregarded Mr Queensbury's investment advice because of the simple and overwhelming logic that he had no money.

It was some time after this that Baxter made a surprising discovery, which he disclosed to Mrs Wilbow as she went about her cleaning.

"You know, I'm not sure I like the smell of that Polygleam any more."

"Well, I'm not throwing it out, I only bought this one yesterday" was Mrs Wilbow's retort.

By the end of that month, Baxter had made a decision. He definitely did not like the smell of Polygleam anymore. In fact, he now found it offensive. Mrs Wilbow listened to his complaint with sympathy.

"Yes, I know what you mean. It's strange but I've gone off it too. We'll go back to the old polish, I think."

Baxter had entered a period when he didn't think his luck could get any worse. These periods were frequent and were assigned adjectives much like an artist as Picasso referred to his 'blue period'. The word currently in use by Baxter to describe his luck was 'stinking'.

As the only paper Baxter ever read was the 'Racing Post', he was quite ignorant of what else was going on in the world. It was therefore with some puzzlement that he listened to Mr Queensbury's unexpected phone call.

"I'm awfully sorry, Baxter, it's a terrible way to repay you for that great afternoon at Goodwood. D'you know my clients still talk about it now."

"Everyone gets lucky occasionally" replied Baxter, mystified by the apology.

"Nonsense! And you deserved better advice than to buy our shares. The truth is Baxter, I did it with the best intentions. We were going great guns then and yet today we've had to issue a profit warning and our share price has gone through the floor. Confidentially, I think you should get out while you can – I can't see the company surviving."

"Oh," said Baxter, suddenly realising that things could have been worse "I never bought any of your shares."

"That's great news and I'm really relieved." Mr Queensbury's voice was much brighter. "The strange thing is our main product was a spray polish that simply flew off the shelves for a time. Then suddenly people decided they didn't like Polygleam and its sales fell off a cliff. I find that difficult to understand, don't you?"

"Yes, I do" said Baxter, not quite truthfully.

THE BEVERLEY MAIDEN

Women had never played a significant part in Baxter's life, although he had to admit that his mother had been quite important at the start. As a teenager, he confessed to having had his moments but it wasn't long before Baxter decided they were a lot of work for little reward. He couldn't ignore them for they were everywhere but the female species held little interest for him unless they were racing fillies. In fact, the last time a lady had aroused his admiration and yearning she'd been French, had chestnut hair and was called Dahlia.

However, had Baxter been inclined towards a female liaison, Beverley Stokes would assuredly have been his choice. Not, however, for her physical attractions which were as hard to find as a good thing in a bumper sprint maiden.

She was a short dumpy woman of about 50 and shaped rather like a bell which, in all probability, had never been rung. She had wispy grey hair and a sprouting of grey whiskers around her chin and mouth. Unfortunately, she also had a badly fitting false eye that wobbled disconcertingly when she looked at you. If all this wasn't enough to curdle any appeal, she smoked a pipe, which she only ever removed when bellowing into conversation with a voice that rasped like a shovelful of coal.

But behind this unprepossessing profile there was a racing genius. Beverley Stokes knew the latest racing mark and form of every classified horse in Britain. She knew its breeding, preferred going, best distance, the course best suited to it and even its idiosyncrasies - in fact, everything to evaluate its winning chance.

The daughter of a small northern trainer, she was christened Beverley when she was born on the same day her father landed a memorable touch at that course. It was sheer good fortune that she hadn't been born a week earlier when he'd landed a similar gamble at Market Rasen.

She was immersed in the form book at an early age when the books of Just William, Billy Bunter and Enid Blyton were substituted by her unscrupulous father in favour of Ruff's Guide to the Turf and the daily delights of The Sporting Life.

As the child prodigy developed into a juvenile genius, the stable prospered and became renowned for its ambushing of hapless bookmakers. There were often no survivors of these attacks with nothing to mark their demise but abandoned pitches and empty hods with stakes through them.

Unfortunately, the father got carried away with success, went for the mother of all gambles in the Thirsk Gold Cup and was virtually ruined when the good thing broke down coming out of the stalls.

When her father retired, Beverley went into racing journalism and eventually became a Jockey Club handicapper. After 2 years of producing so many blanket finishes that photo judges were complaining of eyestrain, she became a professional punter.

Soon she became the doyen among the professionals with an ambivalent attitude to trainer, jockeys and bookmakers alike. She would suddenly turn up at a meeting having not been sighted for weeks. As she approached the front row of Tattersall's, the nervous bookmakers were lined up like figures in a shooting gallery. She'd stop at the first pitch, remove her pipe and jab at a name on the board.

"I'd like £400 at 7 to 2" she'd bark. "You're far too big - 2 to 1 is more like it."

The cringing bookmaker would doff his hat and catapult his floorman to back it back. The second bookmaker would suffer a similar fate.

"Did you hear what I said? Knightsbridge is no more than a 2 to 1 chance."

His response "But I haven't laid it, ma'am" was met with a stinging retort.

"Well, you have now - £200 at the price."

Having executed her business, Beverley would then illuminate the bookies by denouncing whoever made up their tissue. Had he not taken into account the draw or the fact that Knightsbridge came off a strong pace and would get a lead from two confirmed front runners?

Of course, there were occasions when things went wrong as, for instance, when a trainer of Beverley's selection had plotted it up for a future prize at one of the bigger meetings.

"Staking out Woolworths before the shoplift at Harrods, are we?" she would confront the trainer. "I'm reporting you to the Jockey Club."

"She was immersed in form books at an early age"

And she always did. A jockey riding a bad race could also be assured of a blistering accusation of incompetence. "The last time I saw riding like that was in a Thelwell cartoon!" The words would boom around the unsaddling area and was a mortifying experience for any jock.

So Beverley Stokes was a formidable woman. However, despite her foreboding appearance, she was not impregnable to Cupid's arrow and had she seen one she would willingly have stood in its flight path and impaled herself. Sadly, air traffic control was diverting them as if she'd been named the Pyrenees.

Beverley had made Baxter's acquaintance several years earlier but had given up any hope of landing him despite his admiration of her horsepicking talents. Apart from getting rich and leaving a trail of slaughtered bookies in their wake, Baxter decided it was not the path to true happiness although it came tantalisingly close. The thought of a whiskered bride smoking a pipe in his wedding photos was also prejudicial.

Right now, though, Baxter was far too occupied to ponder the absence of romance in his life. For one, there was the recurring inconvenience of a bad run that just now was treating him with the savagery of a woman scorned. If he'd backed the Derby winner in a selling race, it would have fallen over on the last handspring before the winning post. His tipping service was so pathetic that he was astounded that anyone still rang in. In fact, some callers rang in simply to be abusive although Baxter was at least heartened that they were being abusive at a premium rate. His other problem was the sudden appearance of a huge man in his office doorway. Baxter's anxiety was understandable for while disgruntled punters were an occupational hazard, they weren't usually this big.

"Are you the guvnor here?" asked the man.

"That depends on what you want" said Baxter, estimating the stranger to be two sizes bigger than a truck.

"I thought you might have some work for me. I could help you."

"I sell horseracing tips, I don't need any help" smiled Baxter. His relief turned to benevolence. "But have a glass of malt with me."

It seemed that Ben had got Baxter's address from an advert in the racing press and, because he knew a bit about racing, had decided to pop in. His knowledge, however, was quaintly alarming. He talked of 'looking forward to going to Ally Pally', of the old maxim, 'Doug Smith under 8 stone and over a mile' and of 'following George Todd when the money was down'.

Baxter was wondering where Ben had parked his time capsule when it suddenly dawned on him. The scruffy appearance, wanting a job and lack of awareness were all indicative of a recent release from one of Her Majesty's Hotels - and a pretty lengthy one at that.

The next day, Baxter realised that the glass of whisky had signified some contract of friendship to Ben because he turned up again and asked for work.

"I told you yesterday, I don't need any help" said Baxter.

"That was yesterday, what about today?" countered Ben.

It was obvious that Ben was not the brightest of filaments and quite simply wanted to hang around. Apart from admitting he'd just been released, he wouldn't discuss his crime or much else besides.

It was the first day of the July meeting and Baxter was off to Goodwood. He went to the office to leave his racing message. In truth, he should have said something along the lines of 'I haven't got a clue - it's too hard. I'm going to guess a couple of races but if they win, I'll be surprised as you'. Instead, he concocted a message of such flamboyant conviction that it deserved a place in Grimm's Fairy Tales.

Ben arrived as he was leaving. "I'm just off to Goodwood" said Baxter.

"Can I stay here?" asked Ben. "I'll look after the place for you."

Baxter had no time to argue, there was nothing to steal in the office and Ben looked very abject and still very big. He'd worry about it later, pulled a fiver from his wallet and said "Okay, get something to eat."

As usual, there was a big crowd at Goodwood and it wasn't until the second race that Baxter saw the unmistakable figure of Beverley Stokes coming out of Tatts. He suddenly felt brighter for he hadn't seen her for months and to forsake the northern circuit for Goodwood meant that she had one lined up.

He came alongside her. "And so what's the

good thing that brings you here, Beverley?"

She turned around, removed the pipe and greeted him warmly. "How lovely to see you."

She gave him a peck on the cheek that he had to bend down to receive. It was wet but a small price to pay for the information she imparted. Ashtray Cough was the horse and a stone bonking certainty for the frame at 8 to 1. Beverley confided that she'd already had a long one at that price but the beauty was that the market was so strong that the price was still available.

Baxter wasn't messing about with each-way, went in with his head down and took 640 to 80 twice. He rejoined Beverley in the stands and such was the confidence he felt in her presence that he never doubted Ashtray Cough's victory. Nor should he have done for the horse led from start to finish and made the 8 to 1 look like the worst case of overpricing since an early bookmaker went 4 to 1 David against Goliath.

Baxter had seldom felt better. The sun was shining, the course was a buzz of excitement, the sheer exhilaration of winning inflated his whole body with well-being and the presence of bookmaker's money crammed into his pockets was intoxicating. Glorious Goodwood was living up to its name.

Baxter rejoined Beverley and they retreated to the bar to watch the next race.

"Tell you what, Baxter" she drained the remains of a gin and tonic from a glass "I'll drive you back to London and we can catch up with the latest gossip."

"Suits me" said Baxter, whose current

fondness for Beverley would have extended to following her over Niagara Falls.

Soon they were on the motorway in Beverley's open-topped Morgan. Baxter was relaxed, one arm outside the car catching the wind. A Vivaldi tape was streaming out in D major.

"You know Bev, we could have been the Bonnie and Clyde of the turf."

The response was slightly mangled, coming as it did from a piped mouth.

"You didn't want it, Baxter." She paused and then repeated "You didn't want it."

Baxter just smiled happily.

Two hours after leaving Goodwood, they pulled up outside the office.

"I'll just lock up and we'll go to the pub for a little celebration" said Baxter.

He'd forgotten that the two horses on his tipping line had been decisively beaten and he'd also forgotten about Ben who was sitting at the desk in his shirtsleeves. The room looked different.

"I've tidied it up for you" said Ben. "A lot better, I reckon."

It was certainly better but not a lot better, thought Baxter.

"Look, I've had a brilliant day at Goodwood" said Baxter "would you like to join in a celebration? It's all on me."

Ben pulled his coat from the back of the chair, gave a glancing nod to Beverley downstairs and somehow fitted himself into the back of the Morgan.

It was a very enjoyable three hours they spent.

Ben went through the menu and was quiet, Beverley went through an ounce of tobacco and was loud and Baxter went through half a bottle of Macallan and kept singing.

"Ben doesn't drink then - very admirable" said Beverley, observing the bottle of mineral water on the table.

"Of course, he does. My bottle of malt in the office can vouch...." but Baxter's voice trailed off as he noticed Ben's angry glare. He then realised that the big fellow was trying to impress Beverley and that she was flattering him. This was then followed by Beverley announcing that she wondered if she'd drank too much to risk driving back to her hotel in Chichester.

"No problem" said Ben "I'll drive you home." He got up and held out his hands for the keys, which seemed to appear instantaneously.

"What a gentleman" demurred Beverley.

Baxter felt like bursting into song again - it was working out well for everyone.

There was no sign of Beverley for the rest of Goodwood. Ben, too, had disappeared from the scene which was something of a relief to Baxter.

It was more than a month later that he made the alarming discovery. Tidying up his office was a rare occurrence for Baxter but requiring a navigable footpath to his desk, he'd had to pick up several old newspapers and files from around his chair and came across a wallet. Inside it were two out-of-date postage stamps, a bus ticket and, in the note compartment, a yellowed newspaper cutting showing the young but unmistakable face of Ben. The headline above the picture was 'AXE MURDERER GETS LIFE FOR KILLING HIS WIFE'. Baxter's first reaction was that it was pretty lousy poetry. His second was one of panic.

If Beverley was still seeing Ben, she was in great danger. And as he hadn't seen her around - maybe she wasn't around! It was Baxter who'd brought them together. He remembered when Ben had lifted his jacket from the back of the chair. If only he'd found the wallet sooner. He had to contact her at once but realised he didn't know her address or her telephone number. He rang directory - not listed.

His solution was the boxed advert that appeared in the 'Racing Post' the next day.
'WOULD BEVERLEY STOKES – SHREWD JUDGE AND PROFESSIONAL PUNTER – CONTACT BAXTER WITH EXTREME URGENCY'. His private number followed.

It was mid-day when the phone rang.

"Bev, thank goodness' said Baxter recognising the rasping tones. "Is that fellow Ben with you?"

"No, he's actually in the other room clearing out my pipes. I've got over fifty you know but he didn't like my smoking so I've given it up - should have done it years ago. By the way, I never thanked you for introducing me to..."

She'd have rattled on some more if Baxter hadn't interrupted.

"Listen" he said, lowering his voice "you're in serious danger."

"Danger?" said Beverley, raising hers.

"Look, you've probably worked out that Ben's

been inside but the bad news is that he's a murderer." He paused but she said nothing and he went on. "I found his wallet in my office and inside was a newspaper cutting about his trial."

"And who did he murder?" asked Beverley calmly.

"He murdered his wife with an axe. I'm really sorry, Bev."

"Sorry?" said Beverley. "But that's wonderful news!" Baxter was confused and waited for an explanation. Then she added quietly "It means he's free to marry."